Hamfist Over the Trail

The Air Combat Adventures of

Hamilton "Hamfist" Hancock

by

G. E. Nolly

www.HamfistAdventures.com

This book is a work of fiction. Names, characters, places and incidents are either the product of the author's imagination or are used fictionally. Any resemblance to actual persons, living or dead, or to actual events or locales is entirely coincidental.

Cover art by Tony Stencel, http://www.tonystencel.com.

Version 2012.05.22

ISBN **978-0-9754362-3-3**

First Edition: September, 2012

This book is dedicated to American military veterans, past, present, and future.

1

October 16, 1968

As soon as the ENG FIRE light caught my attention, my left hand was moving – almost without my intentional thought – to perform the BOLD FACE actions for an engine fire:

Throttle – Idle

Throttle – Off

If Fire Light Remains On – If fire is confirmed – Eject

In all of our daily pre-flight briefings, the chief instructor pilot had randomly called on one of us, the students, and we were required to immediately respond, verbatim, with the Bold Face responses to whatever emergency of the day he called out. It got to the point that the responses became automatic, pretty much unconscious. It now looked like all of that preparation had paid off.

Time seemed to stand still as I waited to see if the fire light would go out. It was probably only a few seconds, but it seemed like longer, much longer. The light went out.

While I was performing the Bold Face memory items of the Emergency checklist, I was totally functioning on mental autopilot. I felt like I was out of my body, watching this young Lieutenant student pilot go through his actions from above.

But now that the engine fire was out, I was starting to have a visceral reaction. This was my first real emergency, and no matter how many times I had visualized and practiced an Engine Fire procedure, I hadn't expected it to play out the way it did. I certainly hadn't expected everything to seem like it was happening in slow motion.

Now my mouth was dry, my heart was racing, I could feel my pulse pounding in my temple, and I was having a hard time flying smoothly. Being solo sure didn't help.

I was alone in my T-38, leading a 4-ship flight, with my Instructor Pilot – IP – in the number 2 bird. As soon as the ENG FIRE light illuminated, the IP was screaming on the radio.

“Knock it off, knock it off. Lead, your left engine is on fire!”

I acknowledged by repeating the Air Force command for all maneuvering to cease.

“Dingo Flight, knock it off, knock it off.”

I gradually slowed from 300 knots to 250 and rocked my wings, signaling for the formation to rejoin to close “fingertip” formation, with three feet wingtip separation. It was clear to me that my maneuvering was done for the day, but there was no need to ruin it for my wingmen.

"Three and four, you're cleared off into the practice area. I will RTB with number two". The IP in the number three aircraft peeled off with number four, and I watched with a twinge of envy as I envisioned the combat training they would be doing in a few minutes. For me, the fight was over, and it was time to Return to Base – RTB.

We'd been scheduled for an Air Combat Maneuvering practice ride, and I had really been looking forward to finally getting to see ACM first-hand. All of the student pilots in our formation would be progressing on to fighter aircraft after graduation from Undergraduate Pilot Training in a few days, and this would be our introduction to the type of flying we would be doing in the near future. We hadn't received our final aircraft assignments yet, but the four of us in this formation flight were at the top of our class, and we'd all indicated our desire to go to fighters, so it was a foregone conclusion we'd be getting F-100, F-105 or maybe even F-4 assignments to Vietnam any day now. In fact, the assignments should have come in by now.

This was my last scheduled solo flight, and I had been looking forward to returning to base with a nice, tight 350-knot 4-ship flight down initial approach, with a crisp pitch-out and textbook 4-ship in-trail landing. Instead, I would be doing a long, straight-in approach, with the fire department waiting for me to make my emergency landing. Disappointing.

I was starting to calm down again as I headed back to Laughlin Air Force Base. I switched our 2-ship flight over to Approach Control frequency and mentally reviewed the single-engine landing procedure. I started configuring the flight for landing a bit earlier than usual, just to make sure no aircraft systems had been affected by the fire. It was the first time I had ever performed a post-emergency Controllability Check. The absence of any verbal advice from my IP indicated to me that I was probably doing everything correctly.

The scrub brush of the south Texas landscape zipped by at a faster rate than usual on final, since I was flying a higher approach speed due to the inoperative engine and the higher speed due to the lower flap setting. Otherwise, everything seemed pretty much like a normal approach.

A single-engine approach in the T-38 was not that big a deal, really. The only challenge would be the last part, between 500 feet and 100 feet. If the remaining engine were to fail then, I would really be screwed. Too low to bail out or stretch a glide to the runway. They call it a “zero-zero” ejection seat, but what works at zero altitude and zero airspeed won't necessarily work when you're descending at over 800 feet per minute. I unconsciously held my breath.

Luck, I preferred to think it was karma, was with me, and it was an uneventful landing. My IP had been flying fingertip formation on me all the way down final, and executed a missed approach as I rolled out. The fire truck followed me as I taxied to my parking spot, and the crew chief gave me a "thumbs up" after carefully inspecting my bird.

As I finished filling out the aircraft logbook, Airman Folsom, the squadron Admin Clerk, came running up to me. "Lieutenant Hancock, Colonel Ryan wants to see you ASAP."

I knew that Colonel Ryan, the Deputy Commander for Operations – the DO – was informed any time there was an emergency, but I didn't think that he met with every pilot immediately after landing. I guessed he must have really been impressed with my performance, and wanted to personally congratulate me.

I put on my "Joe Cool all-in-a-day's-work" face and went to Wing Headquarters to receive my accolades.

Boy, was I in for a shock.

2

October 16, 1968

Emily, the DO's secretary, ran up and gave me a long, passionate hug as soon as I walked in to the outer office. I immediately looked around to see if anyone else was in view. We were alone. PDA – Public Display of Affection – was seriously frowned upon, and I didn't want to get myself, or Emily, in hot water.

She looked like she might have been crying. “Hamilton! I was so worried!”

Emily and I had been seeing each other, dating, pretty much every day since we'd met at a barbecue at Colonel Ryan's house two months earlier. Colonel Ryan had invited the three top students in our class to his house, and Emily and I had hit it off immediately. She had just been hired as a secretary, right out of college, shortly before we met, and I think I was the first pilot, all right, student pilot, she had ever dated.

“There was nothing to worry about, Emily. It was routine. I'm fine.” I paused. “Colonel Ryan sent for me.” Other than using her first name, I tried to keep it strictly professional, just in case Colonel Ryan could hear us in his office.

Emily knocked on Colonel Ryan's door, and walked into his office. I followed her with my eyes. Damn, she was good-looking! She was petite, about five-two, and had a great figure. Her blonde, shoulder-length hair framed a model's face, and she had a great, bubbly personality. I was really looking forward to seeing her later.

I could hear Emily through the partly open door, "Lieutenant Hamilton Hancock is here to see you, Colonel." I heard a muffled response, and then Emily reappeared.

"The Colonel will see you now."

"Thanks, Emily."

Colonel Ryan rose as I entered the room, and I walked over to his desk, stood at attention, and gave my best Academy salute. "Lieutenant Hancock reporting as ordered, sir!"

Colonel Ryan returned the salute and sat down. "At ease, Lieutenant. Have a seat."

I sat in the stiff wooden chair opposite his desk. It was a chair probably meant to intimidate, rather than provide comfort. I briefly thought of all the poor brown-bars who'd received serious ass-chewing sessions in that chair, and wondered if maybe I'd screwed up somewhere along the way and it was my turn.

“Relax, Ham. You're not in any trouble, but I have some disappointing news for you.” He'd never called me Ham before. In fact, He'd only called me by my first name, Hamilton, once before, when he introduced me to Emily, at his house. Had he learned my nickname from Emily?

“I know you had your heart set on getting a fighter,” he continued, “but I'm afraid that's not going to happen. There are no fighter slots in the assignment roster for your class. I made some phone calls to MPC, but there was nothing I could do for you. Needs of the service.”

I wondered briefly if he really had called his contacts at the Military Personnel Center. Yeah, he had – he was a stand-up guy, and if he said he did something, he did it.

“But sir,” I stammered, “You remember, at the barbecue at your house, you told me I could get any airplane I wanted. You said they did that for every DG.” If I couldn't get the assignment I wanted, why had I worked so damned hard to be Distinguished Graduate – the top student in my class of 48.

“Well, Lieutenant,” the Colonel bristled, “I don't recall the Air Force needing to check with you before they determine their requirements.”

“Let me tell you something about the needs of the service, Lieutenant. I was Top Gun in my class, also. But the needs of the service, in

1944, were for glider pilots. So instead of a P-51, I was assigned to fly a G-4."

He could see from my face I had no idea what a G-4 was.

"I got a total of two hours fifteen minutes of combat time in the air during all of World War II. My glider was towed aloft on June 6th, glided to Normandy with 13 grunts in the back, and then crash-landed in some goddam field, at night, and I became a goddam infantry officer for the next 10 months, while the guys in the class ahead of me were racking up their victories."

"I'll tell you something else, Lieutenant. If something is meant to be, it will be. If it's in the cards for you to get a fighter, at some point you'll get a fighter. I finally got my fighter assignment in Korea, and it was worth the wait." His eyes darted over to a photograph on the wall.

I followed his eyes, and saw a grainy black-and-white photograph of a much younger Lieutenant Ryan, in a flight suit, painting a fifth star on the nose of his F-86, surrounded by a group of equally young Lieutenants holding champagne bottles. Lieutenant Ryan in the photo had a full head of hair and was at least 50 pounds lighter than the balding Colonel in front of me.

But this balding Colonel was an ace!

Colonel Ryan slid a sheet of paper across his desk to me. "Here's the list of available aircraft.

Since you're number one in the class, you'll get your choice of whatever you want from this list. I need to have your selection by close of business today. Dismissed."

I stood up to attention, saluted, did a crisp about-face, and walked out of his office.

Colonel Ryan was a goddam ace!

3

October 16, 1968

I looked at the list of airplanes on the paper the Colonel had given me, and felt like I'd been marooned on a desert island with nothing but ugly women.

There were the usual expected airplanes: B-52, C-141, C-130. And, of course, the Air Training Command airplanes, T-37 and T-38. Then there were two other airplanes I'd never heard of: O-2A and OV-10. These planes were marked with an asterisk, and the bottom of the sheet stated, "*Pipeline Southeast Asia (SEA). Volunteers for this assignment will receive choice of aircraft following service in SEA."

Well, I knew I didn't want a B-52, C-141 or C-130. Someday, after my Air Force career, I would probably want to go to the airlines, and having "big iron" experience would be a plus, but it wasn't what I was looking for at this point in my career. Maybe after I got the "flying a fighter" bug out of my system, but not now.

And I sure didn't want to stay in Del Rio, or anywhere else in ATC, as an IP. While I might eventually want to instruct student pilots, I didn't think I would have the credibility to do it effectively until I had gained some actual operating experience in the real Air Force. It was time to move my career forward, and if I chose an O-2A or OV-10 I'd get to Vietnam, and then I'd get my fighter afterward.

I'd wanted to fly a fighter ever since I was a kid. I'd seen all the movies, heard all the war stories from my dad's friends, and seen the photos of my dad posing in front of his P-51. Dad never spent much time talking about the war, but he had a special look in his eyes whenever he looked up when a fighter flew overhead. I could tell fighters had a special place in his heart right up to the day he died.

Now I had to figure out what the hell was an O-2A and an OV-10. I went to the base library and looked through a book titled *Jane's All The World Aircraft*. Every airplane in the world was shown in the book, just like the title stated. Except the O-2A and OV-10. The O-2A and the OV-10 were so new to the inventory, they hadn't made it into the book.

It was time for me to find an IP with green boots and get some career counseling.

4

October 16, 1968

The inside joke going around the Air Force was that ATC didn't stand for Air Training Command, it stood for Allergic To Combat. Most of the IP force – other than the leadership cadre, like Colonel Ryan – had very little experience in the Real Air Force, whatever that was. A lot of them were plow-backs – guys who had just finished pilot training and then had gone to IP school and stayed in ATC. And some of the instructors had been homesteading on base for almost 10 years. Hell, some of them had been instructing since T-33 days, before the Air Force even had T-38s!

Then there were the guys who had green boots. If an IP had green boots, he had recently returned from Vietnam. That was the only place the Air Force issued green jungle boots. Everyone else had standard-issue black leather flying boots. The guys with green boots had a look about them, it's hard to describe, that said, "Been there, done that".

I found an IP, a young Captain, with green boots, at the squadron break room, having a cup of coffee. I'd flown a training ride with him, and he seemed approachable. I knew he'd flown F-105s, Thuds, in Vietnam, and I was fairly sure he'd know about the O-2A and the OV-10.

“Sir, can I ask you a question about combat airplanes?”

“Sure, Lieutenant.” He motioned to a chair at his table, “Have a seat.”

“Sir, there are no fighters in our block of assignments. But there are two airplanes I've never heard of, the O-2A and the OV-10. Do you know anything about them?”

“Well, I've never actually seen either one, because they're both totally new to the inventory, but I know they're both FAC aircraft. The best I can determine, they're replacements for the O-1. They're basically the same aircraft. Twin-tail FAC aircraft.”

“Thank you, sir”.

I knew what an O-1 Bird-dog was. It was a small single-engine Forward Air Controller – FAC – airplane used for observation and to control fighters during an airstrike. The O-1 had been used in Korea and Vietnam.

In fact, we had an IP in our training squadron who had flown O-1s, Captain Jack Engram. They called him “Jack the FAC”. I searched him out at his desk.

“Captain Engram, can you tell me anything about the O-2A and OV-10? They're both on the assignments bid sheet, and I couldn't find any information about either one of them, other than they're FAC aircraft."

"Well, I'm not really familiar with either one of them, but I'm really surprised the Air Force is assigning Lieutenants to be FACs. Usually you have to have fighter experience to be a FAC. They wouldn't let me be a FAC until I had finished my first tour in F-100s." (Omigosh – this guy's had *two tours* of duty in Vietnam!) "It's great flying. You're going to love it."

I was starting to feel a lot better about my assignment possibilities. I could go to Vietnam as a FAC and control fighters during airstrikes, and then I would get my fighter afterwards. After all, they promised: my choice of airplanes!

I circled "O-2A" on the assignment selection sheet, signed it, and handed it over to Airman Folsom.

I was going to be a FAC!

5

October 16, 1968

I went to Emily's apartment early in the evening, at the usual time. I had sensed that she was really upset over my aircraft emergency, and I wanted to try to make her feel better.

She seemed distracted. I could tell something was wrong.

"What's bothering you, honey?" We had been calling each other "honey" for over a month.

"Colonel Ryan told me about your assignment choices. I'm sorry you couldn't get a fighter."

"That's okay," I responded, "I think an O-2 will be my entry into tactical air operations, and I'll get a fighter when I return from Vietnam."

When I said "Vietnam" she stiffened.

"I didn't think you'd be going to Vietnam," she said. "There's a war going on over there."

“You knew I was planning on getting a fighter assignment. Where did you think I'd be going?”

“You know Sandy, the Wing Commander's secretary?” she asked. “Her husband got a fighter, an F-4 I think, and he was assigned to Europe. Somewhere in Germany. I thought most of the fighter assignments went to Europe.”

I was having a hard time processing this. I had to cut Emily some slack, since she'd only been in an Air Force environment for a few months. But hadn't she been reading the papers? Hadn't she seen the “Air Force Now” movies that were shown every month at Commander's Call? Every “Air Force Now” was about the war, and the role that fighters were playing.

“Honey, our country is at war. That's where I'm needed. The guys who go to Europe only stay there for about a year, then they all cycle to Vietnam. I know you've seen that poster on Colonel Ryan's wall, the one that says 'The Mission Of The Air Force Is To Fly And To Fight'. That's what I've been trained to do.”

“But somebody else could go, and you can go later. I'm sure it's not too late to change your selection. Maybe you could stay here at Laughlin as an IP.”

“Honey, I know this is hard to accept. But, you know, Colonel Ryan went to war, in Europe and in Korea. For all I know he might have gone to Vietnam also. He had loved ones who worried about him, like everyone else who went. They went because that's where they were needed."

When I said "loved ones", Emily's face softened.

"Are you telling me you love me?" she asked.

I hadn't ever gotten up the courage to tell her.

"I guess I am."

She put her arms around me and held me tight. There were tears streaming down her face, and her cheek was warm against mine.

"I love you, too," she said. "I know we'll get through this and we'll be better for the experience."

I kissed her, lightly at first, then more passionately. We sat on her couch and held each other for about an hour, occasionally kissing and saying we loved each other. Then I had to go.

I had to get up early the next morning. It was going to be a big day.

6

October 17, 1968

When I went in to the squadron the next morning, my assignment had already come back: O-2A to DaNang, Vietnam.

Graduation was going to be in 2 more days. I had requested two weeks of military leave, then I would get 3 days travel time to show up at Hurlburt Air Force Base, Florida for O-2 training. After about a month and a half of training I would then get seven days travel time to go to survival school at Fairchild Air Force Base, Washington. Then I would have 1 day of travel time to get to Travis Air Force Base, California, for my port-call on December 25th. I'd be leaving for Vietnam on Christmas.

7

October 19, 1968

Pilot training graduation was a very formal event. This was not going to be the standard Saturday parade. While the 48 of us remaining from our starting class of 70 stood at attention, the rest of the pilot training wing would have a parade "pass in review", and then the Wing Commander would individually present us with our Air Force pilot wings.

I was the first pilot called up to the raised reviewing stand to receive my wings. It was a heady moment. I saluted the Wing Commander and then stood at attention as he pinned my wings on my uniform. Then he shook my hand and I saluted again and left the stand. Each member of our class then was called up, in graduation order or merit, to receive his wings.

After we were dismissed, I removed my wings, broke them in half, and then Emily pinned on another set of wings I had purchased at the Uniform Store the previous day.

The tradition, from well before there was even an Air Force, when it was still called the Army Air Corps, was for a pilot to always break his newly-issued wings in half, for good luck. The pilot would keep one half, and give the other half to a close friend or family member. Only after the pilot dies would the two halves be reunited. I handed the other half to Emily.

I'm not really all that superstitious, but tradition is tradition. And a couple of dollars for another set of wings was a small price to pay for good luck.

Not everyone was into tradition. Don Springer, the number three guy in our class, was one of those. “I don't believe in mumbo-jumbo. I think we make our own luck,” he commented.

And he might have been right. He was certainly an achiever: only a few total points separated him from me in our final grades for academics and flying, and he'd been a straight-A student at the Academy. He'd selected the OV-10, and his orders were quite a bit different than mine. Before going to Hurlburt, he was going to be TDY to Canon Air Force Base, New Mexico, for 3 months. I wasn't sure what that was all about. To each his own.

After graduation Emily and I drove to San Antonio to celebrate. It was a little over a two-hour drive, and we hadn't ever gone there together. We didn't talk a lot on the way. Emily spent most of the time unsuccessfully trying to find a music station that would play on the radio. All she could get was a Spanish Language station playing Mexican music.

When we got to San Antonio, Emily seemed to warm up a bit. We strolled along the River Walk, and walked around HemisFair.

Then we went to see the Alamo. A trip to San Antonio is not complete without visiting the Alamo. I don't know how many times I've been there, but every visit is unique, and I learn something new.

The ghosts of Bowie, Travis and Crockett permeated every part of the Alamo. Here were true American heroes who had crossed that line in the sand, to fight to the death rather than surrender. I wondered if I would have that kind of courage under fire. I hoped I would, but only time would tell.

It was getting dark, and we were both tired. I was trying to figure out how to suggest we stay in San Antonio for the night, when Emily surprised me.

“It's late, and I'd like to see more of San Antonio tomorrow. How about getting a room and spending the night?”

“Sure. Good idea.” I hoped I didn't sound too anxious.

There was a new Hilton Hotel right across from HemisFair, and I got a room with a great, romantic view. We ordered room service, kept the curtains open, and made slow, passionate love well into the night.

8

October 21, 1968

Emily put on a brave front when I had to leave. We held each other, professed our love, and promised to call and write often. She cried a little, and I kissed away her tears.

I'd heard about a program called R&R, and Emily seemed a bit reassured when I told her I'd be seeing her in six months, in Hawaii. She'd never been to Hawaii, and looking forward to our dream vacation together seemed to cheer her up.

I held her one last time, kissed her goodbye and left.

It was easy to get all of my belongings into the trunk of my 1966 Datsun roadster. The bulk of my uniforms and flying gear had already been shipped ahead to Hurlburt, so all I had were my civvies and a few personal items, like my LP records. I also had my blue cardboard pay tube.

"Protect this with your life," the Sergeant at the Pay Desk said. "This tube has all of your pay records, and you can't get paid without it.

Turn it in at the Pay Desk when you get to Hurlburt, sir."

There's an old expression that the Sergeants run the Air Force. It was the truth. We officers signed papers and gave orders, but the Sergeants got things done. This Sergeant looked like he had more years in the Air Force than I had on the planet, and I took his words to heart. I protected that pay tube with my life.

9

October 24, 1969

I lucked out getting a training assignment to Hurlburt Air Force Base, in Fort Walton Beach, Florida. I had grown up in Pensacola, and my mother still lived in the same house where she'd gotten married. My grandmother, my father's mother, lived just two blocks away. I was really looking forward to visiting them.

I had called ahead, and my mother had my favorite meal, meat loaf, for me when I arrived. She was so happy to see me. And so proud when I showed her my pilot training graduation certificate. She insisted on having it framed, and I told her I would like her to put it on the wall in the study, right next to Dad's Certificate of Commission.

Dad and Mom had gotten married on July 4th, 1942, and Dad shipped out to war the next day. He was gone for four years. When I thought about that, I felt like going away for a year, and having a visit with Emily at the six-month point, was nothing compared to what Mom and Dad had gone through. I wished

Emily could meet my Mom and see things in perspective.

I had a nice visit at home. My grandmother came over as soon as she heard I had gotten back, and she was constantly kissing me and pinching my cheeks. She had brought a small, polished, wooden box with her, about the size of a cigar box, and called my mother off into the kitchen to give it to her.

My room hadn't changed since I'd left five years earlier to go to the Academy. I'd heard about some parents turning their kids' rooms into sewing rooms, exercise rooms or recreation rooms when their children grew up. Not my mom. One look at my room and you could believe she still had a teenager living at home. I checked the closet, and my collection of Playboy magazines was still there.

A friend of our family, Phil, who had flown with my dad during the war, came over the second day I was home. Phil was a chain smoker, and reeked of tobacco.

He brought his log book, went through page by page, as he sat next to me, and spent hours telling me war stories. My dad figured prominently in many of them. By his own admission, some of the stories got better with each telling and with each year that passed.

"You know the difference between a war story and a fairy tale?" Phil asked, in his raspy voice.

"No. what?"

“A fairy tale begins 'Once upon a time.’ A war story begins 'Now this is no shit.’ After that, there's no difference.” He lit another cigarette and fell into a paroxysm of laughter and coughing.

I spent a little less than two weeks at home. The time passed quickly, and before I knew it, it was time to leave for Hurlburt. Right before I left, my mother called me into the living room. She was holding the polished wooden box my grandmother had given her.

“Your grandmother gave me this,” she said, as she solemnly opened the box. “She had it in her window the whole time your father was away at war.”

Inside was a small, carefully folded Blue Star flag. The flag was about twice the size of a handkerchief, a white flag with a red border, with a blue star in the middle.

Mom unfolded the Blue Star flag and carefully hung it in the front window.

Then she put her hands on both of my cheeks and kissed my forehead.

“I don't want to be a Gold Star mother. Please be careful.” Then she gave me a long, tight hug.

As I drove away, I saw her wiping away tears.

10

November 6, 1968

It turned out the O-2 and the OV-10 were not the same plane at all. The O-2 was a small, underpowered civilian Cessna 337 that had been modified for military use. It had an engine and propeller in front, like a small light plane, and another engine and propeller in the back. It needed that second engine for performance, due to the weight of all the military modifications.

Those modifications were the addition of numerous communication and navigation radios, plus a rocket pod under each wing. Each rocket pod could carry seven folding-fin aerial rockets, and the large frontal area of the pod increased the aerodynamic drag tremendously. The weight of the equipment, plus the weight and drag of the rocket pods, really affected airplane performance. In fact, the airplane couldn't always maintain altitude when operating only on one engine. The service ceiling when operating with only the front engine was 2000 feet lower than the service ceiling with only the rear engine operating. And sometimes the rear-engine-only service ceiling was under 1000 feet! The only way in or out of the airplane was through the main entry door on the right side of the aircraft. If you needed to get out in a hurry, there was a large red handle just forward of the door. Pulling the handle released the door hinge pins, and you could push the door away from the aircraft. But you would still have to bail out manually. No ejection seat in this baby.

The OV-10, on the other hand, was a big, fire-breathing giant of an airplane. It weighed 10,000 pounds more than the O-2, could fly twice as fast, was fully acrobatic, and had permanently-mounted mini-guns. More important, it had turbo-prop engines and an ejection seat.

Here's the really incredible part: the guys who got OV-10 assignments first went to Canon Air Force Base before going on to Hurlburt, to get checked out in the F-86 and become fully-qualified fighter pilots.

The F-86, although an older jet, was still the “dream machine” for fighter pilots. It had earned a four-to-one kill ratio over the Russian-built MiG-15 in Korea. It was the jet version of the propeller-driven P-51: a fighter pilot's airplane. It was the airplane that Colonel Ryan had flown when he became an ace. And the OV-10 pilots would get to fly it for three months!

Once they got to Vietnam, the OV-10 jocks would be "Category A" FACs, meaning they could perform the more challenging missions, such as Troops-In-Contact, called TIC. Those of us who were in O-2's would be "Category B" FACs, and would not be authorized to conduct airstrikes in support of TIC until we had 300 hours of combat time.

Rather than getting checked out as full-qualified fighter pilots, we O-2 guys would get an "orientation ride" on the gunnery range in the back seat of a fighter. In the FAC world, we O-2 drivers were definitely going to be second-class citizens.

When it was time for my orientation ride, the "fighter" back seat they put me in was an OV-10!

Boy, had I made the wrong choice!

11

November 6, 1968

Okay, so I'd made a bad choice. Nothing I could do about it now. My dad had always said that when life gives you lemons, you make lemonade.

It was time for lemonade.

Flying the O-2 was easy. Employing it for combat was a bitch.

The course consisted of classroom instruction and flying activities. Typically, class was conducted in the morning, and then flying was performed in the afternoon.

The classroom was a large theater-like auditorium, with very comfortable blue velvet seats. It was like a high-end movie theater, and quickly earned the name “the blue bedroom”, because it was really hard to stay awake once the lights went out for a movie or slide presentation.

And there was a lot to learn. We learned about the capabilities of every fighter aircraft, including foreign airplanes, such as the B-57 Canberra that was flown by the Australian Air

Force. We had to learn about all of the different weapons the fighters could carry, and what weapon was best for use against every foreseeable target.

For example, the Cluster Bomb Unit, model CBU-24 or CBU-52, was a great antipersonnel weapon, not so great against a fortified target. The CBU was a large clamshell case, bigger than a 500-pound bomb. Inside the clamshell case were thousands of small balls, each ball containing nail-like projectiles called flechettes. The balls were about the size of baseballs in CBU-24, and about the size of softballs in CBU-52.

When the CBU was dropped, a radar fuse would open the clamshell at a predetermined height, and the balls would scatter in a doughnut-shaped pattern, and would explode when they hit the ground, sending thousands upon thousands of flechettes in all directions. You really didn't want to be on the ground anywhere near a CBU airstrike.

The Mark 82 was the workhorse of the bomb world. It was a 500-pound bomb, and came in two versions: the slick and the high-drag. The slick, as its name implies, was a streamlined bomb, while the high-drag had folding parachute-like metal fins that extended when the bomb was dropped. The Mark 82 was great against hardened targets.

Then there was the AGM-12, the bull pup missile. It had a 250-pound warhead, and was a terminally-guided missile. Once the fighter released it, a rocket motor would fire, and the fighter pilot had a small joystick to guide the missile onto the target. Really great when pinpoint accuracy was important.

Next, we had to learn about enemy defenses, ranging from small arms fire to anti-aircraft artillery, called triple-A, and surface-to-air missiles, called SAMs.

Small arms fire was basically anything the enemy soldier had in his possession. Typically, it was the AK-47 machine gun and whatever pistol the enemy happened to have. The effective range of small arms fire was only a couple thousand feet, so if we stayed a few thousand feet high, it would not be a major factor unless we were unlucky enough to be hit with the "golden b-b".

Triple-A was a major threat, especially for a small aircraft like the O-2. The predominant triple-A threats were the ZPU, the 23 millimeter, and the 37 millimeter anti-aircraft artillery rounds.

The ZPU was a 14.5 millimeter gun, usually four barrels, with a blistering rate of fire of 600 rounds per minute. That's ten rounds every second. It was a really formidible weapon.

The 23 millimeter, called the twenty-three mike-mike, also came in various configurations, from one barrel to four. The four-barrel, the ZSU-23-4, was a real killer. The 37 millimeter was its larger cousin. In all honesty, many of the larger calibers were designed to shoot down the larger, faster airplanes. Anything from a ZPU on up would knock the O-2 out of the sky.

SAMs were the kiss of death for an O-2. The best defense against a SAM in an O-2 was to go to the bar and not fly. The two major SAMs used by the the North Vietnamese were the SA-2 Guideline and the SA-7 Strela. The radar-guided SA-2 was the size of a telephone pole, and was mounted, usually, in a stationary base. It was used to protect fixed targets, such as buildings, and had a range of about 25 miles. Hanoi, the capital of North Vietnam, was protected by thousands of SA-2s. The O-2 didn't fly anywhere near an SA-2 environment.

The SA-7, on the other hand, could show up anywhere. It was a shoulder-fired, portable, heat-seeking missile with a fairly small one-pound warhead, and had a range of a couple of miles. A one-pound warhead would only blow an O-2 into a hundred pieces, instead of a thousand pieces like an SA-2. The bitch of it was, you could find SA-7s virtually anywhere on the battlefield. They were light enough for the average enemy soldier to carry, and easy enough for the average enemy soldier to operate. They traveled faster than Mach 1, the speed of sound, in a corkscrewing flight path. And they homed in on any heat source, such as an aircraft engine.

The mission of the FAC was to be the eyes and ears of the fighter pilot. The FAC was assigned an Area of Operations – AO – and his job was to know the AO so well that he could spot anything out of place or new. This was called Visual Reconnaissance – VR. If he found a target, he would coordinate with local commanders, such as ground commanders and tribal chiefs, and get permission to expend ordnance on the target.

Once he obtained clearance to attack a target, the FAC would call the Direct Air Support Center – the DASC – and get fighter aircraft assigned for the airstrike. The job of the DASC was to make sure that the right strike aircraft and munitions were assigned to the target in a timely manner.

If more than one set of fighters was assigned, the FAC would have to prioritize which set to use first. Perhaps one set of fighters had the perfect ordnance load for the target, but had lots of playtime, while another set of fighters, with less-than-optimum weapons, may have only a few minutes of playtime. It was the FAC's job to determine what order to employ the fighters, and to de-conflict the fighters by making sure they were holding at different altitudes, or in different locations.

Once the fighters were on-scene, the FAC would mark the target, usually with 2.75-inch white phosphorous rockets, called willie petes, and then direct the fighters to place their bombs on target.

Typically, the FAC would be talking to the ground commander on FM radio, talking to the DASC on VHF, and conducting the airstrike on UHF. He had to constantly listen to all three radios to make sure everything was coordinated. Then, he had to keep track of the results of each airstrike: the call sign, type and number of fighters, the munitions, the time on and off target, the location of the target, and the results, called bomb Damage Assessment – BDA. All of this needed to be reported to the Intelligence department at the end of the flight.

During the entire airstrike he had to keep his airplane out of the way of the fighters, keep the airplane in a position to constantly see the fighters and the target, and keep from getting shot down.

Other than that, being a FAC was pretty easy.

12

December 20, 1968

Survival School was not going to be fun. Here I was, getting ready to go to the hot, humid jungles of Vietnam, and I was attending survival school in the frigid northwest. The plan was for us to have a few days of classroom, an escape and evasion – E&E – exercise, then spend another day as a simulated prisoner of war. And then, after that, we'd be taken out into the mountains 30 miles away and have to trek back to base. In the middle of the winter. This was not going to be fun at all.

The classroom part was pretty much what I had expected, and it was actually very interesting. We got a lot of really good information about E&E.

Then it was time to apply it. We were told to go to the BX, buy a package of Kotex pads, and tape them to our elbows and knees. We were ordered to show up at the E&E course at midnight.

The E&E course was simulated enemy territory that we'd have to negotiate in the dark. A special group of instructors would simulate being enemy soldiers trying to hunt us down. At the beginning of the exercise we were each given cardboard tags that we had to carry in our pockets. If we got caught by the enemy, they would punch a hole in the card and let us continue on our way. If we got three holes punched in our cards, we were immediately taken to the POW camp. The hole punch was exactly the same size as an AK-47 round.

A siren sounded, a timer was started, and we were on our way. The finish line was about a mile away, and the course was booby-trapped with trip-wire activated flares. The Kotex pads were to protect our elbows and knees, since we had to crawl the entire course. I managed to avoid setting off any trip-wires, but I got caught once by the enemy trackers. Finally, exhausted, I made it to the finish line.

It had taken me 47 minutes. I was later informed that the school record was 14 minutes, and it had been accomplished by a squad of Marine Force-Recon troops the previous week. That seemed like a pretty good time to crawl a mile in the dark. Then it was pointed out that, in the process, the Marines had disarmed every trip-wire on the course!

After we finished the course, we were immediately imprisoned as POWs. The first thing they did to me was put me in a box. A really small box. To get into the box, I had to squat down with my knees under my chin, and then they pushed me in, hard, and shut the door.

I tried to count seconds to see if I could figure out how long they left me in the box, but I was having trouble breathing and getting a little light-headed, and lost count. I think it was about an hour, but it could have been a lot more. Or a lot less.

Just when I thought I couldn't take the pain in my knees any more, they let me out and put me in a much larger windowless box, probably about the size of porta-potty. Speaking of potty, there was a coffee can in the corner.

After several hours in the box, we were all let out into a “Hogan's Heroes” type POW camp. We were all freezing our asses off, but the physical abuse ended. Time seemed to stand still as we waited for the POW exercise to end. The whole exercise lasted three days.

Finally, it was over. We were sent back to the VOQ and told to report the next day for the trek. But, right before we left, the lead instructor called out the names of all the O-2 pilots in the class, and assembled us in a group.

The lead instructor said, “You have all been identified as candidates for a special class. I can't tell you anything about it now, other than to tell you that attending the class will get you out of the trek. Any volunteers?”

Does a bear shit in the woods? Everybody's hand went up. I didn't care what kind of class it was, as long as it got me out of the trek!

The next day we showed up for the class, and it was a very intensive, super-secret course on things we should do when (not if) we became POWs. Apparently, we O-2 drivers were more likely than anyone else in our survival class to become POWs.

We managed to get out of the trek, but found out we probably wouldn't make it home from Vietnam. Talk about mixed emotions!

13

December 25, 1968

I left Fairchild Air Force Base, drove through the night, and arrived at Travis Air Force Base at about six in the morning. I went right to the Passenger Terminal and checked my bag for the flight to Saigon. I held onto a small bag with civvies – civilian clothes – since my flight wasn't scheduled to leave until about eight o'clock that night, and I didn't want to wear my uniform off base.

In fact, I wasn't allowed to wear it off base to most locations in the Bay area. It was okay to wear the uniform in the local Vacaville area near the base, but everywhere else in the nearby area military personnel were pretty much *persona non grata*.

Especially San Francisco. I had checked with the base Traffic Management Office to see where I could find a reliable garage to store my Datsun for a year while I was in Vietnam. TMO had recommended Morris's Motor Storage, in downtown San Francisco, near the Greyhound bus terminal. I had arranged for a noon drop-off, then I could catch the two o'clock bus back to Travis. That would leave me time for a leisurely dinner at the Officers Club and an easy stroll back to the Passenger Terminal.

I changed into civvies and sneakers and took a long, pleasant drive down Interstate 880 South to San Jose, then up Highway 101 North to San Francisco. Even though I was freezing my buns off, I left the top down. I had no idea how long it would be before I would drive a fun little convertible on a big, clean highway again. I wanted to take it all in one last time.

I decided to see what the big deal was with Haight Ashbury. I had heard about the hippies, and the "make love, not war" movement, and wanted to see what it was all about. I stopped at a gas station on Route 101 and asked for directions to Haight Ashbury and to Morris's Garage.

The gas station attendant glanced at the Laughlin Air Force Base sticker on my front bumper, looked me up and down, and said, "You sure you want to go there? I don't think you'll fit in."

"Yeah," I replied, I just want to see what's going on there."

He gave me directions, and said, "I don't recommend you hang around there too long."

I thanked him and was on my way. I followed his directions and had no problem finding my way.

I parked along the street next to Golden Gate Park, put the top up on my Datsun, and locked the car. Then I walked to Haight Ashbury.

The gas station attendant had been right – I sure didn't fit in there. Long-haired hippies everywhere, pretty much everyone had a tattoo or some kind of piercing, and everyone was wearing garish, flowery clothing. On virtually every corner there was an anti-war poster that read, “Girls Say Yes To Boys Who Say No”.

I wandered around for a little while, endured stares pretty much everywhere I went, and finally headed back to my car. I don’t think I would have felt much different if I had seen an invasion of Martians. Somehow, though, I felt really good about living in a country that allowed that kind of free expression and diversity. I knew you sure couldn't do that in the Soviet Union.

When I got back to my car, I discovered that someone had decided to make an addition to my car. Right on top of the Laughlin Air Force Base sticker, someone had stuck a decal bearing the Peace logo that read “Make Love Not War”.

I tried to peel it off, but it was stuck on pretty firmly. “Footprint of the American chicken” I muttered to no one in particular, and headed for Morris's Garage.

I arrived at Morris's Motor Storage right at noon, and they were expecting me. As soon as I arrived, I knew I was at the right place. They loved cars, and it showed. The floor of the garage was painted grey and shiny, just like an Air Force hangar. They had a complete, organized protocol for storing cars for extended periods. They were going to disconnect the battery, drain the fluids, and put the car up on blocks. When I was ready to pick it up, all I would need to do would be give them at least two hours' advance notice, and they would have the car ready to go, including temporary license tags, since my current registration was due to expire while I was away.

On a grim note, they wanted the name and address of a relative who would be responsible for claiming the car if anything were to happen to me. “It's just a formality. You know, just in case.”

I understood completely. I gave them Emily's contact information.

“You think you can get that Peace decal off for me?” I asked, pointing to the front bumper.

“Sure, no problem. We have a special goo remover,” Mr. Morris replied. “Guess you parked where you shouldn't have.”

“I guess I did. The base TMO said you're pretty close to the Greyhound bus terminal. Can you point me in the right direction?

Mr. Morris answered, “Well, sir, you can go down this long block to the corner, turn right and go two more blocks and turn right again. It'll take about 15 minutes.” Then he gestured to an alley behind me and commented, “Or you can take a shortcut through this alley and it'll take you right alongside the terminal. Five minutes tops.”

I went for the alley.

I hadn't walked very far when I started to have serious second thoughts about walking so far in a dark, unfamiliar alley. There were small alcoves all along the sides, where who-knows-what could be going on.

It was in one of those alcoves that I saw the holdup.

14

December 25, 1968

By the time I came up abeam the alcove, my eyes had already adjusted to the dim light. And because I was wearing sneakers, I wasn't making any noise at all while I was walking. Not even car keys jingling in my pocket.

There was some low-life scumbag pointing a gun at a middle-age man in a business suit who was carrying an expensive-looking attaché case. And the funny thing is, the low-life thug had his back to the alley as he faced the businessman,.

Four years of Unarmed Combat training kicked in without me even thinking about it. Instinctively, I gave a hard kick to his left leg, directly behind his knee, as I reached around and pushed his gun hand toward the sky. I expected a loud BANG any second, but all I hear was CLICK as the guy collapsed like a house of cards.

I grabbed his gun with one hand and his wrist with the other. I gave two sharp twists in opposite directions, and felt his finger and his wrist both snap. He screamed in pain, dropping the weapon like a hot potato. I let go of him and reached down to pick up the gun, and next thing I knew, he was running away like a scalded cat.

The man in the business suit was about my size, five-nine, and looked pretty fit. I suspect if I hadn't come along, he probably could have handled the situation himself. He looked to be in his late forties.

He came up to me and gave me a hug like a long-lost relative.

“Man, you really saved my life! Where did you learn moves like that?”

“The Air Force. Actually, the Air Force Academy.” I flipped open the cylinder of the cheap revolver and saw there were no cartridges. “But I don't think I saved your life. That scum-bag didn't even have a loaded weapon.”

“If you knew what's in this case, you might think differently. Look, my name's Tom Marcos,” he held out his hand, “And I'd really like to do something to make this up to you. And besides, I really like Air Force guys. How about I buy you lunch?”

“I'm Hamilton Hancock. You can call me Ham,” I replied, shaking his hand. “I'd love to take you up on your offer, but I need to catch the two o'clock bus back to Travis. I’m catching a flight to Vietnam tonight.”

"Vietnam. Jeez. How about this," Tom countered, "I'll take you to lunch, and then I'll take you to Travis. My car and driver are just around the corner. First, let's get rid of this," he said, motioning to the revolver. "Do you want it?"

I shook my head, "No thanks."

"Okay, I don't want to just leave it here on the street." Tom picked up the revolver, walked over to a storm drain and dropped the gun through the grate. It hit the bottom with a metallic clang. "Now we don't have to worry about it getting into the wrong hands again. So, how about lunch?"

What the heck, this could be fun. And I could use a little fun. I'd already had a little action.

When Tom said he had a car and driver, he was being a master of understatement. It was a limo, uniformed driver and all.

After we got in and closed the doors, it was apparent that no one outside the limo could see inside through the tinted windows.

Tom opened the attaché case with an air of reverence. "This is why I said you saved my life. My life savings, and the savings of everyone in my company, are right here. I was coming out of the back door of the best diamond cutter in all of San Francisco, probably in the entire country. I always use the back door, because I don't want anyone to see me leaving. I don't think that thug knew what was in this case, or his gun would've been loaded. I guess I was just a target of opportunity."

Tom turned the attaché case for me to see inside. It was filled with small, white, paper sleeves, about two inches square. There must have been a hundred or more. He gently squeezed the sides of one of the sleeves, and several, perhaps up to a dozen, diamonds poured out into his hand. Each one was bigger than the diamond I was planning to someday give to Emily. Easily two carats each, maybe three.

"Are you a diamond broker?" I asked.

"Sort of. I'm in the import-export business, and the Japanese are on a buying spree like you wouldn't believe. And diamonds are their thing right now." He reached into a pocket on the inside of his jacket, pulled out a small silver case and retrieved a card. "Here's my *meishi*."

"Your what?" I asked.

"My *meishi*. My business card. My address is on it. I really want you to write to me with your address when you get to Vietnam"

It was a classy card on thick, bamboo-like stock. One side read:

Thomas Marcos
All-American Import/Export
Shirasaki Building
5-2-20, Akasaka, Minato-ku
Tokyo, Japan
81-3-3311-8222

The back side had what looked like chicken scratches, but I recognized the same numbers.

“Is this Japanese writing?” I asked.

“Oh, yes,” he responded, “To do business in Japan, you need to use both languages.”

“You mean you can read and speak Japanese?” I asked in astonishment.

“Well, it goes with the territory,” he replied nonchalantly. “I'm sure it's no harder than flying an airplane. And it helps to have a Japanese wife.”

“Wow. Your wife is Japanese?”

“Yeah,” he said, pulling a photo out of his wallet, “I really struck gold.”

I looked at the picture. Tom looked younger in the photo, and he was sitting next to a beautiful Japanese woman, and holding a young girl.

“Is that your wife and daughter?”

He nodded.

“They are both so good looking,” I said, and I wasn't just being polite. They were absolutely stunning.

“I lucked out. And, I have to admit, my daughter is a real knockout. You'll probably see Eurasian kids when you get to Vietnam. Almost invariably, they're really good-looking. I'm not that great to look at,” he waved me off as I was about to politely disagree, “but fortunately Samantha got Miyako’s looks. When she was a child, she did some modeling for some Japanese magazines. The media really love *gaijin* in Japan."

"They love what?"

"*Gaijin*. Foreigners. You hungry?"

Actually, I suddenly found myself very hungry.

Tom could see it in my face, and pressed the intercom button to talk to the driver. "Johnny, take us to the Mark."

People like me can't just walk into the restaurant at the top of the Mark Hopkins Hotel and get seated without a reservation. Especially on Christmas afternoon. But Tom could.

We had an awesome wraparound view of San Francisco as we ate the most incredible meal I've ever had. Now *this* was the way to get sent off to combat!

We had a great, leisurely two-hour meal, and talked about everything under the sun. About how Tom ended up in Japan and got into the import-export business. About how I got into the Academy. About Emily. About how I loved flying. About my current assignment, and how I wished I could've gotten a fighter, but this would have to do. It didn't occur to me until afterwards that I had been doing most of the talking.

"You know, Ham," he said, "I know you're going to do great at anything you try. We can't always see the big picture, but there's a cosmic power bigger than any of us that's in control. I don't know what religion you are, but I know that you were put in that alley today for a reason. I pray to that power every night, and I'll be praying for you every night from now on, for your safe return."

We talked on for a while, then it was time to go. You wouldn't believe the looks I got from my Hurlburt classmates when I pulled up to the Travis Passenger Terminal in a blacked-out limousine.

As I got out of the limo, Tom grasped my hand in both of his. "Ham, you have to promise me, you'll keep my *meishi.* Write to me with your mailing address, so we can stay in touch, and call me if you ever get to Tokyo. Have a safe journey." I saw his eyes start to well up as he closed the door. Then he was gone.

And I was on my way to Vietnam.

15

December 26, 1968

The Seaboard World Airways military contract flight to Vietnam had been horrible. I was stuck in a middle seat on a totally full plane, a DC-8. When we stopped for refueling at Hickam Air Force Base, Hawaii, we all deplaned and stretched our legs.

The waiting area was out in the open, and there was the smell of pineapple in the air. I'd been to Hawaii before, during one of my all-too-short summer vacations from the Academy, and the sweet smell brought back memories of a great vacation, a beautiful girl, and a night alone with her on the beach. After about an hour, we were mustered back into the plane.

Most of the people in the plane were young kids. Really young. Maybe eighteen or nineteen. I suspected that most of them were draftees. Almost all of them were Marines.

They were engaging in the kind of horseplay that high school kids do, probably trying to burn off nervous energy as they headed to combat. I wondered how these same kids would be acting when they returned home in a year. I wondered how many would be returning home at all.

The whole trip took about 18 hours, counting the refueling stop. By the time I got to Ton Son Nhut Air Base in Saigon, I felt totally drained.

All of us who finished O-2 training together were on the same flight. Some of the guys would be assigned to Saigon, in the south, some to Pleiku, in the Central Highlands, and some to DaNang, in the northern part of the country. Before we headed out to our final assignments, we had to in-process into Vietnam through Saigon, then we'd receive additional in-country training at Phan Rang Air Base, in the Central Highlands.

In-processing started with standing on the tarmac with our luggage, while the "white mice", the local Vietnamese police, went through our luggage to look for contraband. It was probably only about ten in the morning, but it was already swelteringly hot on the ramp. I was exhausted, dehydrated, and really needed to use a latrine.

We were all standing in a long line with our luggage, and the baggage screener was examining the luggage of the guy at least ten people ahead of me. John Mitchell, another Lieutenant who had gone through training in my class, was right ahead of me. He had been my room-mate at the Visiting Officer Quarters in Hurlburt. He was a good guy, and I knew I could trust him.

"Hey, Mitch, will you watch my stuff? I really need to find a head."

He replied, "Sure. No problem," and I left the line to look for some indication of where there might be some facilities.

One of the local police ran up to me, shouting, "No leave, no leave. You stay." He was pointing back to the line, and his right hand was menacingly resting on the gun on his hip.

"I have to use bathroom. Me want latrine." It's funny how we Americans instinctively use "Pidgin" English as soon as we start talking to foreigners.

"No. No can do. You back in line."

I could see I wasn't going to make any headway with this guy. Then I spotted an American Army Sergeant walking alongside the line of guys waiting to have their bags searched. He had the look of a supervisor.

I caught his eye. "Sarge, can you help me? I really need to use the head."

"Sure, Lieutenant. Follow me." He went up to the Vietnamese policeman who had ordered me back into the line and spoke a few words in Vietnamese. The policeman sheepishly nodded, and the Sergeant and I went off to a small nondescript building at the edge of the ramp.

"Right in there, Lieutenant. Take your time. I'll wait for you out here."

When I finished my business, the Sergeant escorted me back to the line. The baggage screeners hadn't yet made it to Mitch, the guy in front of me.

"Thanks again, Sergeant."

"No problem, sir. We're all in this together. Welcome to Vietnam!" And he was off.

The screening seemed to take forever. The white mice went through every item I had. When they found the hunting knife Emily had given me, they insisted that I couldn't bring it into their country.

"No," I objected, "This was a present for me. I need."

"No bring weapon into Vietnam. Against law."

"It not weapon," I responded, "It survival equipment." There was that Pidgin English again.

It was obvious I wasn't going to win this one. Here I was, coming to help these people fight a war, and they were telling me I couldn't have a weapon! If I hadn't been so tired and hot, I might have put up more of a fight, but I just wanted to get out of the relentless sun and off the ramp that was now so hot I could feel the heat through the soles of my shoes.

The policeman took my knife, seemed satisfied, and went to the next guy in line. I got the impression he was done inspecting my bag once he had found something to take from me.

As we finished clearing our bags, we were marshaled into a large hangar to complete the paperwork associated with in-processing. Although it wasn't air conditioned, we were thankfully out of the sun. It was easily twenty degrees cooler inside the hangar.

The paperwork took at least two hours to complete. We filled out dozens of forms. We had our dog-tags checked to make sure we were who we said we were. We had our shot records checked to make sure our immunizations were up-to-date. And, of course, we completed “In Case of Emergency” contact forms.

I had no way of knowing it at the time, but it would be necessary to use that information for one of us within a week.

16

December 28, 1968

Phan Rang Air Base was a real step up from the misery of Ton Son Nhut. There was a great Base Exchange – BX – and a brand new movie theater. In addition, the Officers Club was being remodeled.

The really ridiculous part was that the U.S. Air Force presence on the base was disappearing. We were going to turn the base completely over to the Vietnamese in another few months, and we had just completed a massive base beautification project. This was my first exposure to the reality that things in the military did not necessarily always make sense.

We – my classmates from Hurlburt and I – had been on base two days already, and were anxious to start pulling our own weight. The flight from Saigon had been thankfully uneventful. We'd all heard stories of cargo planes being shot up by small arms fire while carrying troops, and the C-47 "Gooney Bird" that was transporting us was slow enough to make a really great target.

The seats in the C-47 were center-facing canvas web seats lining the sides of the fuselage. We had heard a story – maybe true, maybe not – about a GI sitting in a C-47 seat when a small arms round came up through the empty seat next to him. He immediately unfastened his seat belt, the story goes, and reseated himself in the seat that had just been hit. His operating theory, apparently, was that there was NO WAY another bullet could go through the same hole! At the time, it made sense. That was before I bought in to the other operating theory that made more sense to me, "when your number's up, your number's up"

We were at Phan Rang to attend our post-graduate training at Forward Air Controller University, otherwise known as FAC-U. Here we would learn to apply, in a real combat environment, what we'd learned at Hurlburt in peacetime.

Phan Rang was an ideal location for an in-country schoolhouse. We would be conducting our training missions over a hostile area, but it was actually considered a low-threat environment. There would be the ever-present small-arms fire, of course, but there were no surface-to-air-missiles, called SAMs, no anti-aircraft artillery, called triple-A, and there were very few actual targets to conduct airstrikes against. Most of the time we would be locating a potential target on the ground, plotting its position, determining it's elevation, and then pretending to conduct an airstrike against it.

And, to make it interesting, we would be constantly targeted by small arms fire.

We were issued the standard equipment before every flight. The survival vest contained a URC-64 emergency transceiver, two day/night flares, first aid kit, signaling mirror, survival knife (bigger than the one the white mice had taken from me), matches, compass and blood chit.

The blood chit was a silk scarf with Vietnamese writing on it, advising anyone who found a downed airman that they would receive a reward if they would help him return to friendly forces. It was a holdover from World War II, when the aviators of the Flying Tigers would have their blood chits sewn into their flight jackets. Back then, the writing was in Chinese.

Next, we received the standard Smith & Wesson .38 caliber revolver and 18 rounds of ammunition. The service weapon was accurate, and the .38 was a good self-defense round, but I wasn't really a fan of having only six rounds before needing to reload. And reloading a revolver in the dark, or when injured, would be a real challenge. We also received an AR-15 automatic rifle. It was similar to the M-16, but had a telescoping stock, which made it much more compact. It fired the same round as the M-16, the deadly high velocity .223, took the same magazine, and had the same blistering high rate of fire in automatic mode.

Finally, we had our back-pack parachutes. This would be my first exposure to flying the O-2 wearing a parachute, and my instructor took extra time to explain the bailout procedure and the process for jettisoning the right entry door in an emergency. He even went into great detail on how to, hopefully, avoid hitting the rear propeller after bailing out. The procedure, he admitted, probably wouldn't always work as advertised.

Some of the exercises we performed were pretty easy, some not so much. Flying the airplane was really a piece of cake. With both engines in line with the fuselage, called centerline thrust, engine-out maneuvering was really easy. And the airplane flew so slow, basically 120 knots, it was easy to project ahead. I had pretty much mastered the aircraft by the time I left Hurlburt, so the flying part was no big deal.

Navigation was different. Unlike the Florida panhandle, there were precious few roads in this area marked on the charts. And, also unlike Florida, where it was sea level pretty much everywhere, the terrain elevation around Phan Rang varied immensely. The only way to determine terrain elevation was to read the notations on the contour lines on the chart showing elevation in meters. The accuracy and safety of the fighter aircraft we would be controlling in real airstrikes would depend upon me providing the exact elevation, in feet, of the target.

To determine the elevation of the target, in feet, I would need to multiply the elevation in meters by three, then add ten percent. It doesn't sound so hard to do this in your head at groundspeed zero, but it's a different story altogether trying to do it in an airplane that's being tossed around by thermal air currents rising from the hot jungle floor, clearing the skies for other aircraft, reading the tiny print on the aeronautical chart, listening to up to three communications radios and watching for enemy ground fire. I started out doing pretty badly, but eventually got the hang of it.

We had a training flight every day, lasting about three hours, and then pretty much had the rest of the day off. Usually, we'd all get together at the Officers Club after the day's flying. The O'Club was situated on a hill, and had a great veranda overlooking the runway. For the brief time we were going to be at Phan Rang, we decided, we'd all get together at the O'Club every day at dinner time and sit on the veranda, drink beer and grade the landings of the F-100s that were coming back from combat missions.

The F-100 jocks, we found out, weren't even active duty pilots. They were from the Colorado Air National Guard, and had been called up for duty in Vietnam. I could visualize it: one day they're having dinner with their families in Denver, the next day they're flying halfway around the world to go to war. All of a sudden,

I had a lot more respect for Air National Guard troops.

One of the big adjustments was getting used to the constant, unrelenting sound of artillery fire. Apparently, Phan Rang Air Base sat fairly close to an artillery base, and Phan Rang was in the line of fire of most of the artillery rounds. Every few minutes we'd hear a loud bang, and then what sounded like a jet plane flying low over our heads. A few seconds later we'd hear the explosion, perhaps 20 miles away. The old-timers on the base said we'd get used to it after a while.

"It's just like the way New Yorkers get used to the sound of the elevated trains that go by their apartments," remarked an IP.

During the brief time I was at Phan Rang, I never did get used to it.

And I was still way too new to get used to hearing about someone getting shot down.

On about our fourth day at Phan Rang, I was scheduled for a late afternoon flight, but when I showed up at Operations, the flight had been cancelled.

The Operations Officer, Major Anderson, pulled me aside. "You were scheduled to fly with Captain Jackson in aircraft 663, but he didn't come back from his flight this morning, so we don't have an airplane or IP for you today. We'll get you rescheduled tomorrow."

“What about Captain Jackson? Who was he flying with? Do we know where they went down?” I had a million questions, and I was more than a little upset with how blasé he was.

“We have several birds in the area looking for any signs of where they might have gone down, but it's pretty hard to spot anything in triple-canopy jungle. We never got a distress call, and there are no beepers. They just didn't come back, and we checked with nearby bases, and they didn't recover at any of the nearby fields.” He rifled through a sheaf of papers, then said, “His student was a Lieutenant Mitchell. Friend of yours?”

It hit me like a ton of bricks. Mitch was down!

17

December 29, 1968

I felt really sick about Mitch going down. What really made me feel awful was that I had just never even gotten to know him. Here we'd been room-mates for over a month, and I didn't even know anything about him. He was just some stranger who showed up in my life and just as quickly disappeared, and I had acted like he didn't even exist. What the hell was the matter with me?

I decided then and there that I would try to really get to know the guys I hung around with. Not necessarily cherish them, but appreciate their individuality. Each was unique, and I wanted to discover that uniqueness. Some were still going to be assholes, but they would be assholes with unique qualities.

I actually got a chance to know Mitch a bit more, in a roundabout way.

The day after Mitch went down, Major Anderson called me back into his office.

"I've been told you were Mitch's room-mate."

"Well, sir, I was," I replied. "Back at Hurlburt we shared a VOQ apartment."

"Okay, then. You'll be his Summary Courts Officer."

"Uh, sir," I stammered, "what's a Summary Courts Officer?"

"You'll be cleaning up Lieutenant Mitchell's personal affairs. You'll make contact with his next-of-kin..."

I froze. "You mean I have to tell his next-of-kin?" I asked incredulously.

"No, no. The Chaplain's office at the base closest to his home of record will do that. Your job is to sort through his mail, see who he's been corresponding with, advise them that you'll be handling his personal affairs. If he owes any money, you'll have access to his bank account to make any payments."

"I'll have access to his *bank account*?"

"As soon as the Staff Judge Advocate signs the SCO orders. Also, you'll need to ship all of his belongings back to his next-of-kin. I don't see a wife listed here. Did he have a girlfriend?"

"Well, sir, I didn't really know him all that well. We pretty much kept to ourselves at Hurlburt." I could feel Major Anderson's eyes drilling into me.

"You know, Lieutenant, you're an FNG, so I'll spell things out for you." As soon as he said "FNG" he saw the puzzled look on my face.

"Fucking New Guy. It usually takes an FNG a while to catch on, so I'm going to help you out."

"Despite what you may have seen in that bullshit John Wayne movie, we're not here to help the brave and valiant people of Vietnam repel Communist aggression. We're not keeping the world safe for democracy. We're not preventing the yellow hordes from invading our country. We're only here for one thing: we're here for each other. We pay attention to what's going in each other's lives, and we do whatever is necessary to help hold up a guy when he's about to fall down."

"Other than our families," he continued, "the people back in the States don't give a shit what goes on here. The fucking anti-war hippies will be spitting on you when you go back home. So we," he gestured toward the flight line, "are your family."

"One other thing, Lieutenant," he added, "I could see by the look in your face yesterday that you thought the world should come to a screeching halt when Bongo 33 went down."

"Well, sir," I answered, "Back at Laughlin we had an aircraft accident in our sister squadron, and the wing had a safety stand-down for two days."

"We've got a war on here, Lieutenant, and it doesn't stop every time we lose a man. For your information, I added three additional sorties last night to fly over the Area of Operations where Bongo 33 was assigned. They orbited the

AO for the entire night, listening for beepers or to see if either of the pilots would come up on Guard frequency. But that AO is the size of Delaware. And it's covered by triple-canopy jungle. For all I know, they could've gone down five miles from the base perimeter and we still wouldn't know it. But we're doing the best we can."

"I understand, sir. I'm going to do the SCO job to the best of my ability." I was hoping he noticed that I caught on to the abbreviation "SCO".

"Good," he responded. "One more thing. When did you go to Clark?"

"Uh," I answered, "I'm not sure who Clark is."

"Wait a minute! Are you telling me you haven't been to snake school?" The veins on his neck were starting to standing out.

"Sir, I really don't understand."

"Goddam it!" Major Anderson was yelling now. "It's the Pacific Air Forces Jungle Survival School at Clark Air Base, in the Philippines. If you haven't been there, it means Mitchell didn't go there, either! So, none of the pilots in your class have been to snake school, right?"

I nodded in agreement. To be honest, I still wasn't really sure what he was talking about.

"That means none of you have been taught a goddam thing about your survival vests. You don't know how to use your URC-64, you don't know how to use your flares, you don't know how to use the tree-lowering device. Do you even know how to use your goddam parachute?"

"Well, sir, we had ejection seat instruction in pilot training."

He was now apoplectic. "We don't have fucking ejection seats, Lieutenant!"

He picked up the telephone on his desk and dialed a number. While he waited for someone to answer, he motioned for me to be seated. I didn't realize until just then that I'd been standing at attention this whole time.

"Hi, Carol, let me speak to the boss." He was no longer yelling. "Hello Colonel, this is Major Anderson, from FAC-U. We've got fourteen Lieutenants from Hurlburt Class 68-55 who got here without snake school." He paused and listened intently.

"Yes, sir," he continued, "I'm certain Lieutenant Mitchell didn't go, either." He looked at me for confirmation, and I nodded. "Yes, sir. Right away, sir." He hung up the phone and dialed another number. "Sarge, I need you to get these 13 remaining FNGs to snake school ASAP. Tomorrow. Make it happen."

He hung up the phone and leveled his gaze at me. "Lieutenant, you are now a proud DG of FAC-U."

I was puzzled. We were supposed to get three more flights. And my performance in calculating spot elevations certainly didn't qualify me for Distinguished Graduate.

“You're done graduated, along with everyone else in your class. Whatever you didn't learn here, you'll learn out in the field. I'll be damned if I let anyone else get his ass shot down without knowing how to use his survival equipment. You'll all be leaving for Clark tomorrow.”

“And Lieutenant,” he continued, “You're still Lieutenant Mitchell's SCO, so I suggest you get on it right away. Dismissed!”

18

December 30, 1969

The previous day had been a blur. The FAC-U admin clerk had given me a Summary Court Officer packet containing a very comprehensive checklist, along with contact information for the Mortuary Affairs Office.

I called the MAO and they explained in detail what I would need to do for Mitch. I would have 45 days to complete all the required duties, they said. When I told them I only had the rest of the day, they pretty much flipped out.

"It can't be done in one day," screamed the Mortuary Affairs Officer. "For one thing, you need to go through Lieutenant Mitchell's hold baggage that was sent on to DaNang."

He was right, of course. I gave it the old college try for the rest of the day. Fortunately, there wasn't much for me to do with the limited personal effects Mitch had brought to Phan Rang. There were no letters, since we our mail hadn't caught up with us yet, so I had no idea who Mitch's correspondents were.

I found his checkbook in his A-4 bag, along with his camera. I held onto those, and inventoried and packed up the rest of his stuff and took the box to the MAO. They said that, under the circumstances, with my leaving for Clark the next day, they would take care of shipping the box to Mitch's next-of-kin.

I'd have to wait until I got to DaNang and looked through Mitch's hold baggage to see what else I needed to do.

I noticed that the camera had a half-finished roll of film in it, and I rewound and removed the roll and took it to the Base Photo Lab. When I explained that I would be leaving the next day, they put in a rush order and had the film developed later the same day.

It was a damn good thing I had the film processed. When I looked at the prints, I saw a selection of photos of our travels since leaving Travis Air Force Base. There was a picture of the Travis terminal, a few photos of the inside of the World Airways DC-8 we had flown in on, a picture of the ramp at Hickam, and a photo of the long line on the tarmac at Ton Son Nhut where we had waited for in-processing.

And then I saw the photos that, if I had left the film in the camera, would have devastated Mitch's family if they ever saw them.

At Phan Rang, like every other air base in Vietnam, there was an "airplane graveyard" alongside the runway. We had all visited and looked at the wrecked planes that had either crashed or been shot down and later retrieved. One of the crashed airplanes was an O-2. As a joke, Mitch had posed for photos on the O-2, like he had just stumbled out of the crashed airplane. He had made a face like he was in pain in all the photos, and in one of the pictures he was hanging out of the cockpit window. That type of joking around was emblematic of the gallows humor that would punctuate our entire time in Vietnam. It had already been pretty much standard for somebody to say, “Hey, if you don't make it back, can I have your stereo gear?” every time a pilot left on a mission. I guess it was the equivalent of “Break a leg” that they say to an actor before he goes on stage. But that kind of humor would sound terrible when taken out of context.

I immediately destroyed the negatives and prints. Yeah, it was a damn good thing I had gotten the film developed.

Early on Monday morning, probably around 0500, all 13 of us in the Visiting Officer Quarters were awakened by a loud bang on our doors. It was Sergeant Williams, the Admin NCO at FAC-U.

“Gentlemen,” he bellowed, “you have 45 minutes until your departure for Clark!”

That was enough time to shit, shower, shave and pack, but not enough time to go to the chow hall. Well, nobody said it would be easy.

We all made it to the waiting bus on time, and were shortly deposited at the Phan Rang terminal. We checked in at the passenger counter, and learned that the C-130 aircraft that would take us to Clark was on a Maintenance Non-Delivery, called MND. They expected to have a replacement airplane around noon, but it was possible that a plane would be ready sooner. We would all need to hang around the terminal, since the plane would be leaving ASAP whenever it was ready to go.

This was my first exposure to the expression, "Hurry up and wait."

We looked around and found a very austere cafeteria, basically donuts and coffee, then sat around in the plastic chairs, waiting. And bitching about waiting. Nobody mentioned Mitch, but everybody was thinking about him.

Finally, around 1100, we were marshaled into a C-130, and were on our way to Clark.

When we arrived, there was a Sergeant from the PACAF Jungle Survival School waiting for us with a military bus to take us to the VOQ. We were given about 15 minutes to check in, then we were whisked off to an afternoon class at PJSS.

As we assembled in the classroom, Major Vandenberg, the chief instructor of the school, welcomed us. "Gentlemen, I apologize for the screw-up that had you going to Vietnam before coming here. I don't know how it happened, but it's history, so let's get to work. We're holding a special class for you, and we'll be giving you two days' worth of instruction today. Your instructor is Sergeant McCoy"

Sergeant McCoy was a Para Rescue Jumper – a PJ – with two tours of duty in Vietnam and numerous actual rescues in South Vietnam, North Vietnam and Laos. On one of his rescues, he had been lowered to the ground to help an injured pilot, and then the rescue helicopter had been forced away by enemy ground fire. Sergeant McCoy spent the entire night nursing the injured pilot and fighting the enemy until another chopper could come back the next day for the pickup. Here was a guy who really walked the walk.

For the rest of the day, we had hands-on instruction about how to use every item in the survival vest. Stuff I never would have figured out on my own. Like which end of the signal flare is for day use, which end is for night.

"The night end has these little bumps," the instructor said, "They feel like little nipples. You feel the nipples at night. Any questions?"

We learned about the beeper. It turned out, the beeper was more than just a sweeping tone transmitted by the survival radio. If the sweep goes from high frequency to low, it means it was set off by an ejection seat. "High to low, just like you're traveling when you come down in a parachute," commented the instructor.

The beeper that is transmitted when the URC-64 is manually placed in the BEEPER position sweeps from low frequency to high.

"You're on the ground, and you want to go up in a rescue helicopter. Questions?"

After the survival vest instruction, we mounted a platform about 20 feet high and practiced using the Tree Lowering Device that was a part of the parachute harness.

"You're going to be operating over triple-canopy jungle," Sergeant McCoy said, "and there's a good chance you'll come down in trees, so you need a way to get down. This TLD will get you down from 50 feet up."

I had to ask the obvious question, "What if we're higher than 50 feet in the air?"

"Well then, Lieutenant," he replied, "you're fucked."

After TLD work, we went to a lower platform, probably about 5 feet high, and practiced our parachute landing falls. We didn't get totally proficient in the PLF, but, what the hell, chances were we'd land in trees anyway.

It was getting dark when we got back in the bus. We expected to return to the VOQ, but the bus drove us off the base and accessed a winding mountain road. Sergeant McCoy noted our surprise.

"I guess nobody told you, you'll be spending the next two days in the jungle," he said with matter-of-fact deadpan.

After about a two-hour drive, we were deep in the jungle. We were deposited at a small campground, with a couple of 2-man tents and a campfire.

The on-site instructor gathered us around the campfire, where there was a large pot with something cooking, along with several small skewers with pieces of meat. He handed us each a skewer, and took one himself.

“Here's your dinner,” he said, as he gnawed at the skewer.

I bit off a piece. It was tough, but it wasn't that bad. Tasted like chicken.

“This is pretty good,” I said. “What is it?”

The instructor smiled. “Gecko.”

I managed to keep the food down. Some of the other guys didn't.

After dinner, we were given mosquito netting and told to find somewhere to sleep. The instructors got to stay in the tents. I looked around and found a place that wasn't too wet, wrapped the mosquito netting around myself, and was soon asleep.

Early the next morning I was awakened by the sounds of people rustling around, and the smell of coffee. When I went to the campground, I noticed that, in addition to the instructors, there were about a dozen people who looked like primitive natives.

They were small, perhaps five feet tall, very dark-skinned, and wearing only loincloths.

"These are local negritos," the instructor announced. "They are indigenous natives to the Philippines, and are the best trackers in the world."

"During World War II," he continued, "they were the best weapon we had in the Philippines. They would sneak into Japanese camps at night and slit the throats of every other sleeping soldier. You can imagine the effect that had on the enemy, to wake up and find the guy next to him dead."

"Today they're going to show you how to survive in the jungle, and how to evade, and tonight you're going to try to hide from them and they're going to find you."

He didn't say "Try to find you", he said "Find you." I was determined to prove him wrong.

We spent the day learning about how to find food and water sources in the jungle, how to avoid dangerous animals, and how to hide. I paid rapt attention.

As night fell, it was time for hide-and-seek. We each went off in different directions, wearing survival vests they had given us. We were simulating being downed aircrew members trying to escape and evade while waiting for rescue.

Along with our survival vests, we were issued three plastic dog tags to put on our dog tag chains. Each tag was really a form of payment. When a negrito would find any of us, he would retrieve one of our plastic dog tags and later redeem it for a bag of rice.

When the siren sounded in the morning to signal the end of the search, I had successfully evaded the searchers. I popped a smoke from my signal flare to show my position, and carefully worked my way out of the thicket. It took about an hour for me to extricate myself.

It turned out I was the only one in our group to have successfully evaded the negritos. Finally, I was a DG again!

When we all gathered at the campsite, we were rewarded with a real breakfast. The instructors had cooked bacon and eggs for us, and we all chowed down like we hadn't eaten in a week.

After breakfast, we piled onto the waiting bus to go back to Clark. Sergeant McCoy was at the front of the bus, talking to someone on a walkie-talkie.

When he finished, he announced, “Gentlemen, your flights to Vietnam will depart tonight. You'll have your Travel Authorizations waiting for you at the VOQ.”

When the bus deposited us at the VOQ, I went into the Billeting Office and got my TA. I would be leaving on a C-130 for DaNang at 2300 hours. I went back to my room and looked at the bed I hadn't slept in since I arrived.

I took a well-needed shower and decided to take a nap. I set the alarm that was in the room, and as I drifted off to sleep if occurred to me: I'd be spending New Year's Eve, like Christmas night, in an airplane!

19

January 1, 1969

When I arrived at DaNang it was about three in the morning. I had no idea where I was supposed to go, or what I was supposed to do. All I knew was that I would be in the Covey Squadron. Every FAC had his own call sign, and the call sign for each pilot in our squadron was Covey plus an identifying number. I was to become Covey 218.

To my surprise, there was a Major at the terminal holding a sign with the names of the three of us who were assigned to DaNang.

"Welcome to DaNang, welcome to Covey Squadron, and Happy New Year!" he beamed, "I'm Walt Walters, the Covey Squadron Ops Officer."

We took turns shaking his hand.

"We're really glad to see you guys. We've been under-manned for over a month, so you guys will be getting all the flying you want. Come with me. I'll take you to the squadron first, then we'll get you set up in your hooch."

We followed him to a beat-up Jeep. It was a standard GI Jeep, and it looked like it had been left over from world War II. It might have been.

The squadron was surprisingly abuzz with activity for the middle of the night.

“We operate around the clock here, so there will always be someone at the squadron if you need anything,” he remarked. “The boss will be here in about an hour.”

Major Walters called out to a Captain who was arranging some photos on the far wall. “Hey, Speedbrake, come and take care of our FNGs.”

The Captain walked over and introduced himself, “Welcome to DaNang. I'm Speedbrake Kane. How about you guys come over here with me, so I can take your picture. Then I'll show you around the squadron.”

We followed Speedbrake over to the wall that had a large Covey Squadron plaque, a picture of Snoopy on his doghouse making a rocket pass. We individually posed by the plaque as Speedbrake took a few pictures of each of us with his battered Nikon F.

“I'll get these processed as soon as the base photo lab opens, and then you'll be on the wall with the rest of the guys.”

I looked over at the wall that had all the pictures. They were arranged into the four units, called Flights, that comprised the squadron. Altogether, there were about 90 photos, with about 25 each in A Flight, C Flight and D Flight. There were only 15 in B Flight.

"Why is B Flight so small?" I asked.

"We've had a run of bad luck with B Flight. Two guys got shot down and never made it back, one was injured in a rocket attack and medically evacuated back to the world, and we had three DEROS last month. So all three of you will be in B Flight. The B Flight Commander is Major Withers. He's on R&R right now, so you won't get to meet him for about a week."

Lieutenant Johnson, one of the other FNGs, asked, "What's a DEROS?"

"It's when you go back to the world. It stands for Date Eligible to Return from Overseas. It's an official military acronym. It will be exactly one year from when you left the States. When's your DEROS, Johnson?"

"Christmas."

A Lieutenant, wearing Navigator wings, overheard him as he walked by. "If I had that long to go, I'd walk through a minefield," he quipped. "Wearing snowshoes! I guess that would make you our FNGs. Welcome to DaNang. I'm Clink Clinger."

We were in the midst of making our introductions when the siren sounded.

Everybody in the squadron stopped what they were doing and quickly walked out the side door. They didn't scramble, but they didn't take their time, either.

“Come with me,” Speedbrake said.

We quickly followed him out the side door of Covey Ops and into the nearby bunker. It was a structure about ten feet high, with plywood walls surrounded by sand bags, and corrugated steel sheets topped with sand bags on the roof.

Several of the guys inside had flashlights, and I could see that the interior of the bunker was pretty austere.

I could feel my heart racing, and I was glad it was dark enough that no one could see how scared I was.

“You'll get used to this,” Speedbrake commented. “The gomers lob rockets at us pretty much every night. Not too much of a big deal, really. They're not very accurate.”

Just as he said that, we heard a deafening BANG, followed a few seconds later by an even louder explosion. After a few more seconds, there was a slightly softer report, and then a final explosion from what sounded like far away. About a minute later the siren stopped.

“That's why DaNang is called Rocket City,” remarked a Lieutenant. “I guess they were welcoming you. Hi. I'm Balls Balser.”

In the dim light, I could make out a very young-looking, tall Lieutenant. We made our introductions, and followed everyone back to the Ops building.

"One last thing about rocket attacks," Speedbrake added. "If you're in your rack, don't get up to go to a bunker, just roll out and get under your bed. The guys who get hurt in rocket attacks are the ones who stand up."

When we got back inside, Major Walters said, "I'd like to visit with each of you separately for a few minutes. Lieutenant Hancock, come with me."

We went into the small office with the sign "Operations Officer – Major John Walters" on the door, and he motioned me to a leather chair.

"Too bad about Mitchell," he said. "I hate it when an FNG gets shot down. We didn't even get a chance to know him."

He looked through the pages of a manila folder he was holding. "Looks like you were DG in your pilot training class. We don't get many of those."

"Sir," I asked, "I noticed the sign on the door said your name was John, but you introduced yourself as Walt."

"It's this way, Lieutenant. Everybody here has a moniker. It's kind of like a nickname. We typically use their real name to come up with something that sounds similar, or else we use something unique to come up with a name. You met Balls Balser in the bunker. And, of course, you met Speedbrake, our squadron welcome officer. Walt Walters seemed like a natural for me."

"What kind of name is Speedbrake?"

"Oh. During his first tour he was flying thuds. He came off a target over Hanoi and was rejoining his flight with a lot of overtake. He extended his speed brakes to slow down for the rejoin, and forgot to stow them. He almost ran out of gas on the way home because he needed so much power to stay in formation. He picked up the name Speedbrake after that, and it stuck. It even followed him here."

He paused for a moment, deep in thought. "I guess we'll call you Hamfist."

I was dumbfounded. "Hamfist" was an aviation term that referred to a person who's a really poor pilot. "Sir," I stammered, "I'm not sure why you're calling me that."

"Well, the way I see it," he answered, "we can either call you Handjob, because it sounds like Hancock, or Hamfist, because it sounds like Hamilton. Your call."

It didn't take me long to decide. "I guess I'm Hamfist."

Major Walters got up, opened the door to his office and stood in the doorway. "Gentlemen," he called out. When Major Walters started to speak, everyone pretty much stopped what they were doing and looked our way.

"Let's have a hymn for Hamfist Hancock."

As if on cue, in unison, everyone in the room intoned, "Hymn, hymn, FUCK HIM!" Then everyone cheered.

I was now officially a Covey.

20

January 1, 1969

We hung around the squadron for about an hour more, getting to know the guys who were there. They were all O-2 drivers, since the OV-10s only flew in the daytime.

"We have O-2s and OV-10s," explained Fish Fisher, "and the OV-10s don't fly at night, so everyone here is an O-2 pilot."

"Why don't the OV-10s fly at night?" I asked.

Balls was walking past us, overheard my question, and ventured, "Because they're pussies!"

Fish continued, "Well, they have a big bubble canopy, and it causes a lot of reflections that make it almost impossible to see targets at night or use a starlight scope. The gomers can hear the difference between an OV and an O-2, and they send their movers on the trail if they hear an OV at night."

He was using terminology I hadn't heard before. "What's a starlight scope?" I asked, "And what the hell is a gomer?"

"You'll see the starlight scope on your first night flight. It's basically a telescope that amplifies light so you can see in pretty much total darkness. And a gomer is, well, one of the bad guys. It's an official acronym the Intel people use for Guy On Motorable Enemy Route. We pretty much call all the Vietnamese gomers," he answered. "But not to their faces."

Suddenly, everyone in the room stopped talking. They didn't snap to attention like when a general enters a room, but they did stop talking and stand up. The Squadron Commander, Lieutenant Colonel Ryder, had arrived.

He spotted us three FNGs right away, and came over to us and introduced himself. It was obvious from the ensuing conversation that he had read our personnel files and gotten to know something about each of us.

He looked over at me and said, "Sorry to hear about your friend Lieutenant Mitchell."

I silently nodded.

He spotted Major Walters in the corner. "Hey Walt, let's have Speedbrake drive these guys over to the Covey hooch and get them settled in."

When he heard his name, Speedbrake came over. "C'mon guys," he said, "Let's get you settled in."

We piled into the squadron Jeep and headed out across the base to the Covey hooch, about two miles away, with Speedbrake driving.

"You're not going to *believe* the Covey hooch," he remarked. "Probably the best quarters in all Vietnam. Certainly the best at DaNang. A lot of jocks think Gunfighter Village is better, but we have individual air conditioning units, and they only have central air."

"Gunfighter Village," he continued, "is where the F-4 jocks live. When the F-4 first came out, it didn't have a gun, only missiles. When they finally had a centerline gun pod for the bird, the first unit to receive it was the 366th, here at DaNang. From that time on, everything they did was Gunfighter this, Gunfighter that. All of their aircraft use the call sign Gunfighter. I'd say up to half of the flights we control in the daytime are Gunfighters."

I was a bit confused. "I thought we only fly the O-2s at night."

"No, not exactly," he responded. "The OV-10s only fly during the daytime, but we fly around the clock. We have squadron aircraft departures every three hours. The OV-10s take off at 0900, 1200, and 1500, and we take off at 1800, 2100, 2400, 0300 and 0600. It takes about an hour to reach our AO. We stay on target for about two hours, then we RTB. So each mission is about four hours."

"Actually," he said, after thinking what he had just told us, "the OV-10's get to the AO in about a half hour, so they're on target about three hours. Anyway, this way there's always overlap over the target area with previous and following FACs."

"And," he added solemnly, "you don't have to wait very long for an on-scene commander if you go down."

We pulled up outside an austere building. It looked like a standard military barracks. When we entered, I could see that there were individual rooms on each side of a long hallway. About halfway down the hallway was a short connecting hall that connected to another long hallway. From above, the building looked like the letter "H". The latrine and showers, and a washer and dryer, were located in the short cross hall.

Our names were already on the doors to our rooms, written on sheets of paper and attached with thumb tacks. I went into my room and put what little items I had on the empty bed. It was apparent that I would be sharing a room with Fish.

The room was really pretty nice. Probably better than the VOQ at Hurlburt. Fish had his side of the room decorated with fold-outs from Playboy Magazine, and there was a large Akai reel-to-reel tape deck on the desk near his bed. A window air conditioner was running, keeping the room comfortably cool. Fluorescent light fixtures were in the ceiling, and there was a table lamp on each desk. The two beds were on opposite sides of the room.

I unpacked my A-4 bag and put my clothes in the dresser on my side of the room. I expected my hold baggage would arrive in the next day or two, with the rest of my belongings. I put my personal items in the desk on my side of the room, and placed the photo of Emily on the right corner of the desk. She could watch me while I slept.

After about fifteen minutes, we met up with Speedbrake, as agreed. It was probably obvious from our faces that we weren't all that impressed.

“You probably don't think this is so special, right?” Speedbrake asked.

“It's not bad,” I replied.

“Let me tell you what you'll see if you visit your friends who aren't Coveys, even the Gunfighters. They'll be lucky to have running water, they'll be damned lucky to have toilets, and they'll be super-lucky to have air conditioning. Guys, this is about as good as it gets!”

Just then the telephone in the hallway rang. Speedbrake answered it, listened for a few seconds, said “Thanks” and hung up.

“That was Ops. They said there's going to be an Arc Light about ten miles west of the base in five minutes. Follow me.”

We walked around to the north side of the building, where there was a ladder leading up to the roof of our hooch.

"Let's go up to up topside to get a good view."

We all climbed the ladder and gathered on the flat rooftop. There was a low wall about three feet high surrounding the roof, and there were some outdoor tables and chairs. Obviously, this was a gathering place of sorts. I wondered, briefly, how they had gotten the furniture up there with only a ladder.

Speedbrake pointed up, way up, in the sky. "Here they come!"

I followed his hand and saw, barely visible, a line of B-52s spaced about a mile apart, flying in trail formation. They must have been well above 20,000 feet.

And then I saw what looked like an endless barrage of bombs falling from the airplanes. At first, they looked so small I could hardly tell they were bombs.

"Look at that!" Speedbrake yelled. "One hundred six fucking bombs on every one of those babies! Wait till you see them hit!"

And then we saw the first set of bombs strike the target area. And then the next set of bombs. And the next. The bombing just seemed to never stop. I tried to determine how many B-52s were on the bombing run, but I lost count after about twenty.

This was not pinpoint bombing, it was total annihilation carpet bombing.

About thirty or forty seconds after we saw the bombs hit the target area, we started hearing the explosions and feeling the concussions. Even at this distance, the overpressure was immense. I was really glad there was a low wall surrounding our patio. It gave me a feeling of security that I wouldn't get blown off the roof.

“This is the nearest Arc Light I've seen. The bad guys must really be getting close to base,” Speedbrake commented. He looked off to the west at the immense cloud that had formed over the target area. “I don't think they'll be coming back for a while.”

21

January 2, 1969

The previous day I had gone on a walk around the compound to see what was near our hooch. We were located over a mile from Gunfighter Village, and had pretty much everything we needed, other than a BX, right in our compound. The chow hall was a stone's throw away, and the O'Club was only a block further.

The O'Club had a big sign that read “DOOM Club”. It was an acronym for DaNang Officers Open Mess. Large green footprints were painted on the sidewalk outside the club, put there by the rescue helicopter squadron.

The HH-53 helicopters that performed the Search and Rescue – SAR – mission were called Jolly Greens. The large footprints signified the Jolly Green Giant, like the vegetable brand. The Jolly Greens flew as slow as the O-2, and they ventured into the most hazardous locations in North and South Vietnam, as well as Laos, without hesitation. It was pretty much a certainty that Jolly Green drivers never bought their own drinks at any O'Club in Vietnam.

I got up at 0300 hours and went to the chow hall across the street from our hooch. They were open around the clock, and breakfast was a super deal, at 27 cents for all you can eat.

The reason I was up so early was that Major Walters had notified me the previous evening that he wanted me to fly the 0600 mission. Although the briefing was scheduled for 0430, I wanted to get to the squadron a little early, and it would take me probably 30 minutes to walk the two miles to the squadron.

Walking two miles was no big deal. Walking two miles in the sweltering heat was something else. I was sweating profusely when I walked into Covey Ops and felt the blast of cool air.

I arrived exactly on schedule, and met with the Combat Tactics Instructor Pilot who would be with me on my flight. The CTIP on this flight, Boss Boston, was a pilot I had known at Laughlin. He was two classes ahead of me in pilot training, and had only been in Vietnam a little over three months. After three months, he was already considered an “old head”.

For a fully-qualified combat-ready pilot, the typical schedule rotation would start with the early evening mission, the 1800 launch. After a week of flying the 1800 mission, the pilot would then cycle to the 2100 mission for a week. Each week the pilot would cycle to the next later departure until he flew a week of the

0600 launches, then he would get a week off from flying. During the week off from flying, he'd typically have some administrative duties around the squadron and maybe a day or two off.

Flying the 1800 and the 0600 missions gave the O-2 pilots a chance to see the AO in the daytime, which was important for situational awareness. The schedule of mostly night flying, however, made it difficult for the O-2 pilots to perform a lot of normal activities, like making doctor and dental appointments, taking care of administrative functions at base offices, and shopping at the BX when we were not flying, since we would usually be sleeping during the daytime.

Our mission planning started with a briefing from the squadron Intelligence Officer, a junior Captain. He issued us plastic-covered "1-to-50" charts, with potential targets marked in grease pencil. The 1-to-50 designation meant that one inch on the chart represented 50,000 inches on the ground.

The 1-to-50 was the perfect chart for a FAC aircraft flying at a groundspeed of about 120 knots. Significant geographical features were easy to see on the chart, but it wasn't too detailed. A smaller scale chart would show more detail, but it would be too easy to "fly off the edge of the chart", requiring additional charts. As it was, we needed to carry numerous charts to cover the entire AO. The next larger scale was the 1-to-250, which would have been easier to carry, but didn't show enough detail for FAC duties.

"You'll see that, after a few weeks, you'll know our AO like the back of your hand," Boss noted. "I was told you had to leave FAC-U early, so we have a lot of stuff to brief that they didn't teach you at Hurlburt."

And brief me he did, non-stop, until it was time to head out to the airplane for a quick preflight and launch. To be honest, I felt a bit overwhelmed, but Boss said that's how he felt a few months ago, and it would come together pretty quickly.

The airplane was parked in a fortified revetment. Each airplane had its own separate revetment. We conducted the preflight inspection, and it was pretty standard, other than the rocket pods. They were full: seven 2.75-inch folding-fin white phosphorus aerial rockets, called "willie petes", in each pod. In training, we had only flown with four willie petes, two in each pod. The weight and drag of fourteen rockets would really affect airplane performance.

After the preflight inspection, I started to get into the airplane.

"Not yet, Ace," Boss remarked, "Time for the most important part of the preflight." He was standing by the edge of the revetment. He had unzipped his flight suit from the bottom and was urinating on the revetment.

"I got into this habit of pissing on the revetments before every flight," he continued. "It brought me luck. Then, about two months ago, Major Walters told me to get my ass into aircraft 443 and get airborne ASAP for a high-priority SAR. So I jumped into 443, didn't even have time to preflight. Naturally I didn't have time to piss on the revets."

"I went to the target, it was Delta 43, and that nine-level gunner nailed my ass as soon as I got over the target area. I managed to bail out a few miles away from Delta 43, and the Jolly Greens actually got to me before they picked up the survivor. But I decided then and there I would never again fly without pissing on the revetments."

I stood next to Boss and peed on the revetment also. Then we climbed into the airplane. Boss got into the left seat. That surprised me, since I had been flying from the left seat throughout all my training, and would always be in the left seat once I got checked out.

"This will be your dollar ride," he said, referring to the Air Force tradition of having an easy first ride in a new airplane. "I'll take the left seat today, and you can pretend you're my FAN." Seeing the puzzled look on my face, he continued, "You may have noticed some guys in the squadron have navigator wings. They're our Forward Air Navigators. We use them at night to look through the starlight scope to spot targets."

DaNang had two long, parallel north-south runways. As we taxied out for takeoff, I heard the distinctive roar of the two J79 engines of an F-4. I instinctively looked over toward the runway, and didn't see an F-4. Instead, I saw a plain O-2, without rocket pods.

"What's that about?" I asked.

"Oh," Boss answered, "that's an O-2B, a Bullshit Bomber. The Bullshit Bombers have huge speakers and fly around at night playing funeral dirges. The gomers are real superstitious, and if they get scared enough they come over to our side."

"More superstitious than you?" I asked, thinking of his ritual of peeing on the revetments.

"Oh, lots more. The funeral sounds are part of the Chieu Hoi Program. They also drop Chieu Hoi leaflets."

"What's Chieu Hoi?" I asked.

"I think it's Vietnamese for 'Time to surrender' or something like that," he answered. "The Bullshit Bombers use their tape players and speakers to make themselves sound like F-4s on takeoff. That's what they do for fun."

22

January 2, 1969

We took off on runway 35-Right and turned east to climb out over the ocean. I hadn't flown in the O-2 with fully loaded LAU-59 rocket pods before, and was really surprised how sluggish the climb performance was.

"That's China Beach down there," Boss remarked as we passed over the coast. "It's going to seem like the hardest part of the mission is getting to the AO. We need to contact DaNang Arty on fox mike and find out if we conflict with any artillery fire."

We tuned the FM transmitter to the frequency for DaNang Artillery Control. They would be able to inform us of all artillery firing in the area, including shells coming from navy ships that were firing at targets inland.

"DaNang Arty, this is Covey 212, request arty coordinates." Covey 212 was Boss's call-sign.

The response came back rather quickly. "Covey 212, we have fire from DaNang 050 for 17 to 260 for 28, from DaNang 130 for 6 to 280 for 21, and DaNang 245 for 15 to 290 for 34. Max height 5000 feet."

The points were radial and distance from the DaNang TACAN. We plotted the points on our local area chart, and it was obvious we couldn't proceed directly to our target area, to the west, unless we flew right through the lines of fire.

"Okay," Boss asked, "what do you think we should do?"

"Well," I answered, "it looks like the only way we can get to the target area is by proceeding south for about twenty miles, and then heading west."

"Yes, and that would probably make sense in a jet," he responded. "But in an O-2, it will take us an extra 15 minutes of flying time, and that will limit the amount of time we have in the AO. How about we just fly through the arty – it's a big sky."

"You're the boss, Boss," I replied, with a really uneasy feeling in the pit of my stomach.

As soon as we were finished talking to DaNang Arty, Boss tuned the ADF receiver to the frequency for Armed Forces Radio Service, and I heard the strains of a Beatles song.

"I want you to get used to listening to more than one radio at a time. The best way to do that is to practice listening to AFRS on ADF"

We turned and headed out to the west, continuing to climb until we reached 7000 feet.

Every now and then we'd hear what sounded like a jet going by.

"Another arty shell that missed us," Boss commented.

Big sky indeed.

Our AO was central Laos, called Steel Tiger. During the briefing Boss explained that it was a free-fire zone, and we'd always be able to find a target to employ fighters on. Being a free-fire zone meant that we didn't need to get clearance to expend on any target we would find. Anything we saw would be fair game.

Sometimes, Boss explained, we'd have fighters assigned to us in advance, with a scheduled rendezvous time and place. Today, however, we'd just have to contact the airborne Direct Air Support Center. The call-sign for the DASC was Hillsboro for daytime flights, Moonbeam at night.

"Hillsboro and Moonbeam operate as the DASC for all of Steel Tiger. They're in a C-130 out of NKP, and can get us any air assets we want on fairly short notice," Boss said.

We flew west for about 50 minutes. The terrain kept getting higher and more rugged, with dense, triple-canopy jungle covering virtually every landmark, other than rivers and lakes. The only way to navigate was by reading contour lines on the 1-to-50.

Boss pointed off to the right. “That's the A Shau Valley. There are 10,000 NVA down there looking at us right now.”

Ten thousand North Vietnamese Army soldiers watching us right now! Again, I had an empty feeling in the pit of my stomach.

“Let's light 'em up a little,” Boss suggested. “I'm supposed to show you our alternate marking procedure, anyway.”

He reached into the pocket behind my seat, and grabbed two smoke grenades. He wrapped a large rubber band around the handle of one of them.

“Open your window,” he said. He then handed me the smoke grenade with the rubber band. “Hold it outside the window.”

I held the grenade outside the window. I hadn't realized how strong the slipstream was at 120 knots.

“Pull the pin and drop the grenade,” he instructed. “Be sure to hold it well outside the window. If you drop it into the airplane, we're really fucked.”

I pulled the pin and dropped the grenade.

“Now do the same with the other grenade, the one without the rubber band,” he said.

This time, when I pulled the pin and dropped the grenade, the grenade handle immediately snapped into the ARM position.

We started a hard turn to the left, then, after 90 degrees of turn, reversed turn to the right.

"Now," Boss noted, "you see that smoke trail? That's from the grenade without the rubber band. In the daytime, if the fighters have a hard time seeing you and the target area, sometimes you can use a grenade to draw a vertical line in the air."

"Now let's see where the smoke grenade landed."

After a brief wait, we saw a plume of white smoke billow up from the jungle.

"If you're ever winchester on rockets, you can still mark targets," he remarked. "We always have at least four smoke grenades in the pocket behind the right seat."

"One question," I asked, "What do you mean winchester?"

"That means the aircraft is fully expended, out of ammo. The fighters say it all the time to tell us they don't have any more ordnance."

I guess it was due to this being my first flight into a combat area, or my apprehension about all those eyes looking at us, but I really had to urinate.

Boss could see me squirming. "Got to piss, right? Happens all the time." He reached into the pocket behind my seat and produced a plastic pouch containing a sponge. "This is a piddle pack. We always have a stash of them in the seat pocket. I think you can figure out how to use it."

He was right – I figured it out with no problem. As I filled the piddle pack, it expanded to about the size of a football. “Now what do we do with this?”

“Well, Hamfist,” Boss remarked, pointing out the window, “if we can drop grenades on the gomers heads, we can drop bags of piss also.”

I tossed the bag out the window and it disappeared into the slipstream. I had a momentary mental picture of an NVA soldier walking through the jungle, when a bag of urine lands on his head. Not even close to payback for that rocket attack.

“What's that clicking sound?” I asked. I had been hearing it ever since we had gotten over the higher terrain. It sounded like someone repeatedly opening and closing the cap on a Zippo lighter.

“Oh,” Boss said, “That's small arms fire. You can't see it in the daytime. Not really anything to worry about, since we're pretty high. At night it looks like a bunch of strobe lights going off. You'll see.”

“I don't really sweat the small arms fire,” he continued. “It's the heavy stuff they have on the trail we have to worry about. ZPU, ZSU 23-4 and 37 mike mike. We can't really see that in the daytime, either, unless it gets really close. Your first night flight will water your eyes, though.”

Boss pointed off toward the distance in the direction of north. There was a confluence of several rivers that joined into the shape of the letter “H”. He pointed it out on the chart. “That's Tchepone. It's right outside of our AO. You don't want to go there. It's a good place to get your ass shot down.”

I nodded silently.

Boss tuned the VHF to Hillsboro's frequency. “Hillsboro, Covey 212 entering the AO.”

Hillsboro responded, “Roger Covey 212. We have plenty of air assets if you need them. Two flights of F-4's, a two-ship of F-105s, and we may be getting some Navy A-7s that weather diverted from their primary target.”

“Roger.”

Below us we could see a brown dirt road winding in and out of the jungle. Boss pointed down at it, and then pointed to the corresponding area on the chart.

“That,” he said, “is the Ho Chi Minh Trail.”

23

January 2, 1969

The Ho Chi Minh Trail – the trail - was the long artery that ran from Hanoi, in North Vietnam, through Laos and branched out to arteries that continued into South Vietnam. It was the way the NVA resupplied their troops and brought the 122 millimeter rockets they would fire at us and at the civilian population.

Back at Laughlin, Jack the FAC had told a bunch of us student pilots about the trail when we were in pilot training. He'd said he liked to picture some poor coolie carrying a rocket on his shoulder, all the way from Hanoi. "He slogs through the jungle, fighting off insects, reptiles and tigers, getting his ass bombed day and night, and finally gets down to Saigon, after about two months. He hands the rocket to his commander. The commander sets it up, fires it off and then says, 'Okay, Nguyen, go back to Hanoi and get me another one!'" Every time told the story he laughed so hard it looked like he was crying.

The airplane noise was noticeably louder with the window open, but we could still communicate with no problem on interphone. Still, Boss had raised his voice a bit ever since I opened the window.

"That's Delta 27, and marks the eastern end of our AO. The DASC knows these delta numbers, and can find the air assets that are closest to us when we call for fighters."

As we entered the AO, Boss reached up to the fuel selectors in each wing root and moved the switches to AUX.

"We've been flying long enough to make room for the bypass fuel to go back into the mains."

Although I hadn't flown with fuel in the AUX tanks in training, I knew that the O-2 fuel system always returned some unburned fuel from the injection system back into the main tanks. We needed to make room in the main tanks for this returned fuel before we used any fuel from the AUX tanks. That was the reason we burned from the main tanks first.

Boss handed me a pair of binoculars, as he maneuvered to place the trail on my side of the plane. "Take a look, and tell me if you see anything."

We flew along for about thirty minutes, with the trail on the right side of the airplane. At Hurlburt, they had shown us how to do Visual Reconnaissance, but hadn't told us how disorienting it can be to VR with binoculars.

Every now and then, I'd see something that looked like it might be a target, but when I took the binoculars away from my eyes, I lost sight of the exact location.

Boss could see I was having trouble. "Here," he said, as he handed me what looked like a shoebox with binocular eyepieces on one end and some switches on the top. "Zoom in with this button, and when you see something of interest, put it on the cross-hairs and then press this button to turn on the gyro stabilizer. Then zoom out and your target will still be in the cross-hairs. You can even take your eyes away from the gyro-box and when you look back in, the target will still be in the cross-hairs."

I practiced with the gyro-stabilized binoculars for a while and started to get the hang of it.

Then I saw my first truck.

"There's a truck down there," I said excitedly, "right by that horseshoe bend."

"Let me see." Boss took the gyro and studied the target. "We're at Delta 71. Looks to me like this is a flak trap. See how the truck is sitting mostly in the open, not even camouflaged? They want us to bring some fighters in to attack it. When we're all in the area, they'll open up with triple-A. Mark it on the map, and we'll report it to Intel."

I could see I had a lot to learn.

We followed the trail west, to where it intersected a major north-south route. The Mekong River followed that branch to the north and south as far as the eye could see. Just north of the intersection, the river made large switch-back.

“That's Delta 49, also called the Dog's Dick.”

To be honest, it didn't look like a dog's dick to me, but it was a memorable bend in the river, and a memorable name.

We turned north to follow the trail, and in the distance I could see prominent white cliffs along the west bank of the river.

Boss pointed in their direction. “Those cliffs are the most prominent feature of Delta 43. Like I said, there's a 9-level 23 millimeter gunner there, the guy that nailed my ass, and I don't recommend you get too close until you have a better feel for the area.”

I had noticed we had begun slow jinking, swerving unpredictably from side to side, as we started heading north. Not anything violent, just heading changes every few seconds.

“You don't want to fly straight-and-level when you're around here.” Boss advised, “Just do some unpredictable S-turn maneuvering all the time.”

We headed off toward the west, and well off in the distance I could see an airfield.

“That's Saravane. It's an Air America base called Lima 44. I wouldn't call it a really secure area, because it's still in Laos, but if you get hit, it's closer than Ubon. If it's not an emergency and you just need to recover somewhere other than DaNang, I recommend Ubon, because it's in Thailand. I'll tell you right now you can't get back over the mountains to DaNang on one engine."

I made a mental note.

We headed back to the East, staying to the north of the east-west portion of the trail. I was practicing VR with the gyro binoculars in wide-angle view, when I saw a piece of the jungle move across the road. I wasn't sure what I was seeing. I turned on the gyro and zoomed in to get a closer view.

As I zoomed in, I could discern that there was a group of soldiers, perhaps twenty, perhaps more, crossing the trail, holding a large sheet of camouflage netting over their heads. If I hadn't been looking right at them at the time, I never would have seen them. I put the gyro stabilizer on its highest setting, so I wouldn't lose sight of the target.

"Boss, I think I see a gathering of people down here at three o'clock."

Boss put the aircraft into a right bank and said, "Let me see."

I handed him the gyro binoculars, which were still pointing at the target. Boss zoomed out, then zoomed back in, and quickly plotted the point on the chart.

"Good job, Hamfist. You found us a target."

Boss became all business. He switched the transmitter over to VHF.

"Hillsboro, Covey 212. We need air assets at Delta 54. Prefer CBU."

"Roger, Covey 212. I'm sending a four-ship of Gunfighters with Mark 82s, ETE five minutes, and in fifteen minutes you'll get a flight of F-105's, call sign Boxer, with CBU-24. Strike frequency Echo."

Boss showed me the frequency card, pointed to the fifth line, labeled "Echo", read across to the designated frequency, and tuned our UHF. In the meantime, he was reaching into the large pocket on the leg of his flight suit for his KAK wheel, the authentication device we would use to confirm that we were, in fact, talking to friendlies.

"I'd prefer to use CBUs against these gomers, but it's just as well we blow the covering off their hiding place with the Mark 82s first, then we'll use the CBUs. So it won't hurt to put Gunfighter in first." Just then, Gunfighter checked in on strike frequency.

"Gunfighter 21 check."

"Gunfighter 22."

"Gunfighter 23."

"Gunfighter 24."

"Covey 212, Gunfighter 21 flight of four fox fours, Mark 82 slicks, ETE three minutes, ten minutes playtime."

“Roger, Gunfighter 21. When you get to the rendezvous point, set up a left hand orbit and look for a bend in the river that looks like a pair of tits. Authenticate mike bravo.”

“Roger, entering the orbit now, have the tits in sight. Authentication zulu.”

“Okay, look near the cleavage, I'm in to mark.”

We rolled into a 120-degree bank, pulled the nose through and entered a 30-degree dive with the target directly ahead. While we were rolling and diving, Boss was setting up his armament switches to fire from the left rocket pod. As we reached firing parameters, he picked off two rockets in rapid succession, and then pulled up sharply to the right, then banked left to look at his marks.

“Shit,” he said on interphone. “I'd like to tell you I purposely missed the target, but it was just a lousy mark.”

“Covey, I have two smokes on the ground.”

“Roger, Gunfighter, I have two marks oriented east to west, fifty meters apart. I want you to put your bombs thirty meters due south of the western mark. Target elevation,” Boss quickly scanned his plot on the map, “is 4600 feet. Wind is from the south at ten. Run in from north to south with a break to the west. I'll be holding off to the east. Cleared in hot.”

“Lead's in.”

We were heading north now, and Boss was watching the airstrike through his left side window. I craned my neck to watch.

Lead's bombs were close, but no cigar.

"Okay, two, I want you to put your bombs ten meters short of lead's. Cleared in hot."

It looked to me like number two's bombs were right on target.

"Number three and four, put your bombs five meters short and five meters long of number two's bombs. Cleared in hot."

Just as he finished his transmission, another call came over the strike frequency.

"Boxer flight, check."

"Two."

"Hello, Covey, Boxer flight of two fox 105s, CBU-52, approaching rendezvous, angels 23, ten minutes playtime."

"Roger, Boxer, set up an orbit to the left, and let me know if you see our airstrike. Authenticate whiskey delta."

"Foxtrot."

"Gunfighter flight is winchester."

"Roger, Gunfighter, you're cleared to RTB. I had you on target at 45, off at 53. One hundred percent on target, BDA RNO. Good job. Thanks." Boss handed me a grease pencil, and, on interphone, said, "Write down what I just gave him. Put it right there, on the side window."

We heard Gunfighter leaving.

"Thank you, Covey. Gunfighter flight, button three, go."

"Two."

"Three."

"Four."

Boss was back on strike frequency. "Boxer flight, I want to bring you in from east to west with your CBU. Target elevation 4600 feet. Do you still have the target area, or do you want me to mark it?"

"Lead has the target. I'm ready to roll in. Am I cleared in?"

"Cleared in hot. I'll be off to the south. I want you to pull off to the right, to the north."

I could see Boxer Lead on his run. He released his CBU, and then there was a small flash under his airplane.

"Was that triple-A?" I asked.

"Naw. That was his CBU opening up."

Then I saw a large donut-shaped twinkling pattern along the ground, right where I had seen the soldiers.

"Good hit. Aim for the same spot, number two. We'll keep dropping on the same area until you guys are winchester."

Boxer flight gave us one more pass each, then were winchester and headed home. They had gotten all of their CBU right on target. Boss gave them the BDA, and I dutifully copied it onto the side window.

I was disappointed that all of our BDA had been RNO – Results Not Observed. It was obvious that no one could have lived through a pounding like that. I had been hoping to get a feel for how many gomers had been Killed By Air – KBA.

"Can't we just estimate how many gomers we killed?" I asked.

"No way. RNO is RNO. Unless we see dead bodies, or count body parts and divide by four, we don't have KBA. Never, I repeat, never make up KBA. When we debrief Intel, it's going to look like all we did was turn trees into toothpicks. You and I know better."

"Got it. Hey, Boss, how soon are we supposed to RTB?"

Boss looked at the clock, looked at the fuel gauges, and his eyes widened.

"Shit! We've stayed here too long. I don't know if we have enough fuel to make it back to DaNang."

"How about Ubon?" I asked.

"At this point, it's about the same distance. Shit, shit, shit."

We jettisoned our rocket pods and started a shallow climb.

"Crack open your door, and lean out the cylinder head temperatures to max," he instructed. "Tighten your parachute harness and be ready to bail out. But don't go until I give you the word. If the engines quit, I don't want to bail out until we're away from the A Shau Valley, unless we've descended below 1500 feet."

I really had to pee again, and reached back and grabbed another piddle pack. But somehow, I was too uptight to use it. I just couldn't go.

DaNang was in sight now, and we had declared a fuel emergency and requested direct overhead the base. We arrived over DaNang at 5000 feet and flew a flame-out pattern, which would put us in a good position to land if the engines did fail at any point.

Overhead at 5000 feet, downwind at 2500 feet, base leg at 1200 feet. Piece of cake. We landed, and the rear engine failed just as we taxied in.

We didn't say much as we taxied in to park at the revetments. After we shut down and secured the plane, we copied the strike information I had written on the window in grease pencil to a debriefing sheet. Then we went to Intel and gave our debriefing.

"One last thing," Boss said, as he opened a cabinet in the squadron break room. He brought out a bottle of Johnny Walker Black. "We're entitled to mission booze."

It turned out that there was actually an Air force regulation that stated that crewmembers were entitled to one ounce of whisky after each combat sortie.

“We usually save up our ounces until we get full bottles, then trade with the marines for boxes of steak and lobster. Today, I think we'll just drink it.”

“I'll drink to that,” I replied. I still had to pee.

24

January 2, 1969

There was an A-4 bag and an A-3 bag on the floor of my room when I returned from flying, along with a cardboard box containing some letters.

Mitch's hold baggage had arrived and had been automatically forwarded on to me. Apparently the MAO had been on top of things. The bags were waiting for me in my room at the hooch when I came back from the 0600 mission.

It was tough looking through the belongings of someone I hardly knew. Fortunately, for me, there was nothing especially remarkable or personal in his bags. Just uniforms and civvies. I put it all in a box to send to his next-of-kin.

Mitch's mail was also waiting for me to look through. There were about ten letters, held together with a thick rubber band.

The first one I opened was his American Express bill. Funny, I hadn't pictured Mitch as an American Express type of guy. The bill was for $43.89. I dug out his checkbook and wrote a check for the total amount. In the signature block I signed, "Hamilton Hancock, POA John Mitchell," as the MAO had noted in the SCO instructions.

There were a few letters from cousins and other relatives. The Mortuary Affairs Officer told me that, under no circumstances, should I be the person to inform any relatives of Mitch's status, so I just put the letters in the box with his clothing, to later send to his next-of-kin.

There was a letter from a girl, I couldn't tell if it was his girlfriend or just a friend from college. I sent the form letter of notification to her, along with my contact information.

Finally, there was a letter from his mother. It had been written on December 28th, three days after we left for Vietnam. It was written in real ink, not ballpoint pen, with the kind of careful cursive script that indicated the letter had meant a lot to the author:

"My Dearest Son,

Words can't describe how proud your father and I are of you. You were always the one we counted on whenever we needed anything. I know it wasn't easy for you to help us on Second Lieutenant pay, and we really appreciate it.

Your sister really feels bad about the way she treated you right before you left. I don't think she really meant all the things she said, I think her boyfriend put some of those anti-war ideas in her head. Right after you left, she got in a big argument with him and broke up with him, and I heard he ran off to Canada. Good riddance, I say. She's better off without him. She said she's planning to write to you soon. She wants to send you some cookies she's planning to bake, but she's worried they might go stale before they get to you. What do you think?

We love you very much. We think of you every day, and we pray for your safe return every night. Please stay safe!

Love,

Mommy and Daddy"

I put down the letter from Mitch's mother and cried uncontrollably.

25

January 7, 1969

I was signed off for day solo operation after my first mission with a CTIP, and flew four missions in rapid succession.

At first, I pretty much retraced the route I had flown with Boss, just to become familiar with the area. Since I was solo, I kept the trail off the left side of the aircraft, so I could VR with the gyro-stabilized binoculars.

Slowly but surely, I started to get comfortable with the AO and started picking up on hints of enemy activity. Subtle things like finding wheel track marks leading off into the jungle, indicating a possible truck park.

There was always air support whenever I requested it from Hillsboro, and I put in airstrikes on anything and everything that looked like it might be a target. I was gaining experience quickly, but not getting anything in the way of significant BDA. Mostly, making toothpicks.

By the end of my fourth solo day mission, I had gotten to the point that I didn't feel nervous any more.

When I finished my Intel debriefing after that mission, I finally met my Flight Commander, Major Withers.

“You must be Hamfist,” remarked a tall, balding Major. “I'm Warthog Withers, your Flight Commander. Let's have a chat.”

He motioned to some chairs in the corner of the small squadron lounge. “Have a seat. Sorry I couldn't be here to welcome you when you arrived. I just came back from R&R in Honolulu.”

“Sounds like fun.”

“It was. My wife and kids met me at the Hale Koa, and we had a great time. It was really tough getting on the airplane to come back here.” He paused. “Enough about me. I hear you're all checked out for day operations. Do you have any questions, or concerns?”

“Not really, sir. I'm just trying to learn the AO as quickly as I can. I've put in a few airstrikes, but haven't gotten any real BDA yet.”

“That's pretty normal. A lot of our missions are pretty much hours of boredom punctuated by moments of sheer terror. It's really important for you to keep doing exactly what you're doing right now, getting to know the AO intimately. You're going to be like the neighborhood cop on the beat, who can spot something that's out of place because he knows the area so well."

"I want to give you the Withers theory on risk. Flying combat is kind of like walking along the top of that wall that goes around the top of our hooch. You've been up there, right?"

I nodded.

"Well, if I told you to walk around the building along the top of that wall, the first time you did it you'd be in a lot of danger, because you wouldn't be used to walking along a narrow ledge. You'd be real careful, but your risk would be pretty high. After about twenty times, your risk would be decreased a lot, because you'd get the hang of walking along a ledge, but you'd still be real careful. After about a hundred times, your risk would actually be higher, because you'd be so comfortable walking on a ledge that you'd get cocky, and prone to making careless mistakes."

"Flying combat is a lot like that," he continued. "Most of the guys who get shot down are either on one of their first or last scheduled missions. You wouldn't believe how many guys just never return from their champagne flights. Keep that in mind. There's nothing out there worth dying for."

"Yes sir," I answered, "I understand."

After I left the squadron, I walked back to the hooch, took a shower, and went to the Doom Club to have dinner. I saw Speedbrake sitting alone at a table, and asked him if I could join him.

"Sure," he answered, "Have a seat. How's your flying going?"

"I'm starting to feel pretty comfortable. Haven't gotten a lot of BDA yet, though."

"It comes in spurts. I've gone for weeks with nothing at all, then had five missions in a row with incredible secondaries. It'll come."

I was a little hesitant to discuss the subject of nicknames, but Speedbrake seemed really approachable. "Can I ask you a personal question?"

"Sure. Shoot."

"Does it bother you that once you pick up a nickname, it follows you around? I'm not really all that thrilled to think I'll be called Hamfist for the rest of my career."

Speedbrake chuckled. "Well, it may be a big Air Force, but it's a small tactical community. You'll always be running into somebody from your past life. You're going to be Hamfist for a long time. Get used to it. Hell, I feel like Pierre the bridge builder."

"What do you mean?"

Speedbrake feigned a French accent. "I beeld a hundred breedges, but do they call me Pierre the breedge beelder? No! But I suck *one leetle deek*, and I am forever called Pierre the cocksucker!"

He continued, without the accent, “I was a pretty good fighter pilot. My bombs were always right on the fucking target. One mission, I was coming off the target in pack five, and there, right in front of me, was a fucking MiG-17. I don't know who was more surprised, him or me. Almost by instinct, I armed up the gun and blew his ass out of the sky. I was so pumped! I rejoined my flight with a ton of smash, and had to go to idle and extend my brakes just to keep from overshooting. All I could think about was that MiG I had just killed, and I forgot to stow my boards. It took a ton of power to stay in formation, and I pissed away a lot of gas.”

“I expected to pick up the nickname Killer Kane, or something like that. Instead I became Speedbrake. Just like Pierre.”

26

January 23, 1969

There was a really good MARS station at DaNang. MARS was an acronym for Military Affiliate Radio Station, and it was a great way to get a free phone call back to the States.

The base MARS station would place a radio call to a ham radio operator in the States, and the ham would get a phone-patch to the number we wanted to call. The MARS operators would try to get through to a ham close by the place we were calling, but sometimes there would be long-distance charges involved.

Besides the cost, there was another big problem with making a MARS call. Everyone in the MARS station, including all the people waiting to make calls, could hear your call, since the incoming signal was played over a loudspeaker.

Both the MARS operator and the ham operator needed to listen in to the conversation so that they would know when to switch their radios from "transmit" to "receive". At the end of every transmission, the person talking needed to say, "over".

More than once I was in the MARS waiting room and heard, "Will you marry me? Over," and then, usually after a heart-wrenching delay, "Yes. Over." And we'd all cheer.

I had called Emily a few times already, and she seemed a bit uneasy knowing that other people were listening to our conversations. And she had a really hard time saying "over", so there were often long pauses during our conversations.

But, eventually, she got to the point where she would say, "I love you. Over."

I placed a call to her at Colonel Ryan's office right before I went to fly. Due to the time difference, it was often hard to time our calls properly. It was early evening in Vietnam, so it would be morning in Texas.

We made small talk, and I had an opportunity to remind her that we were getting closer to the time when we'd get together in Hawaii. I'd already been away from her for a month. In all honesty, the time had gone by really quickly because I'd been so busy. I hadn't had all that much time to sit around and think about how much I missed her, and, although I really wanted to hear her voice, I was making the call more for her benefit than for mine.

After the call, I went to the squadron for my scheduled 2100 departure. This was going to be my first night flight. Like my first day flight, I'd be in the right seat, performing the duties of a FAN.

Boss was my CTIP again, so we dutifully peed on the revetments before flying. Our ordnance was different from a daytime load. In addition to rockets, we had one station, under the right wing, outfitted with parachute flares, and another station, under the left wing, with ground marking flares.

The parachute flares had arming wires attached to the mounting pylon. When a flare was dropped, the wire would pull a pin out of the flare's fuse and start a 30-second timer that would trigger the deployment of a parachute and the ignition of a very bright, very hot flare that was several million candlepower in brightness. When we dropped a flare, it would light up the target area for about five minutes.

The ground marking flares, called “logs”, weren't as bright. The would free-fall to the ground, then illuminate for about thirty minutes. Typically, we would drop two logs at a time, usually on a cardinal heading, and then talk the fighters to the target by reference to the two lights on the ground.

The flight to the AO was uneventful. We both went to great lengths to not mention anything about our previous flight together. I think we were both pretty embarrassed. I sure was. On the way to the AO, Boss showed me how to operate the starlight scope. He also pointed out the many flashes on the ground that indicated small arms fire.

The first order of business was to adjust the focus to the “infinity” position. The best way to do this was to point the scope at a distant bright light, such as a star or one of the many flares illuminating different parts of South Vietnam. Since the city of Hue, off to the north, was usually under flare illumination most of the night, it was easy to find a light source to focus on.

As we got to the AO, I started practicing looking at the trail with the starlight scope. It was amazing how well I could see features with the scope when everything just looked pitch black to the naked eye.

Suddenly, I saw one, then another, very bright light directly below the right side of the airplane. The lights appeared to be fairly stationary, but they were slowly moving apart.

“Hey, Boss, I've got two bright lights that are staying in the same place, but getting further apart.”

“Shit!” he shouted, “they're tracers!” as he violently banked the airplane to the left.

As soon as he raised the right wing, the tracers zipped by, close enough to touch. They made a slight popping sound as they went past us. And, through the open window, I smelled the distinctive odor of cordite. It reminded me of a fireworks display I had seen from close up when I was a kid, when the wind had blown the smell of the fireworks in my direction. Shortly after they missed us, the tracers exploded with a loud report.

"That was a 23 mike mike," Boss commented. Mark our location on the chart, and we'll report it to Intel. There haven't been any reports of 23's in this area before."

We looked around, and couldn't determine where the ground fire had come from. Boss wasn't satisfied to let it go.

"We need to get some air and see if this guy opens up again."

He switched over to Moonbeam's frequency on VHF.

"Moonbeam, Covey 212."

"Covey 212, go ahead."

"Covey 212 in the area of Delta 51. I need air immediately. We have an active 23."

"Roger, Covey 212, we're sending Magpie 11 flight over to you. Strike frequency Delta."

"Roger. Thanks."

Boss pulled his KAK wheel out of the leg pocket of his flight suit, and listened up on strike frequency.

"You need to go to the BX and get yourself one of these," Boss remarked, as he held up a small rectangular flashlight. "It's a Sanyo Cadnica."

"What's so special about it?"

"It's a very low illumination level, so it won't blind you or ruin your night vision. Also, you can use this switch" he held up the flashlight so I could see the sliding switch on the side, "to change from white to red light. You'll need the red light for most of the things we do, like using the KAK wheel, but you need the white light for reading contour lines on the map. Watch."

He moved the sliding switch to turn on the red light, and held it over the map. The orange contour lines on the map totally disappeared. Then he slid the switch over to white light, and I could see the contour lines again. Yes, I definitely needed a Cadnica.

After a few minutes, we heard Magpie flight check in, and Boss had them authenticate. They sounded different from the fighters I'd heard previously.

"They're Aussies," Boss explained. "The Magpies are B-57s out of Phan Rang. You're playing FAN tonight, so be sure to keep track of all of our information. Just like before. Start time, end time, target coordinates, ordnance, BDA, the works."

"Got it."

When Magpie flight was overhead, they couldn't see us.

"Not a problem," Boss transmitted, "I'm going christmas tree now."

With that, he turned on every light on our airplane: navigation lights, rotating beacon, and landing light.

“Okay, Covey, we have you in sight.”

“Roger,” boss transmitted, “set up a wheel to the left and I'm going to see if I can get this guy to open up on us. If he starts firing, you're cleared in hot from wherever you are at the time. Just keep me informed of your direction.”

Boss rolled into a 120-degree bank and brought the airplane nose around to the target area in a 30-degree dive. He armed up the rocket pod and fired off a willie pete.

Firing a rocket at night was a totally different experience from daytime. The rocket motor left a trail of sparks all the way from the airplane to the ground. The rocket hit the ground with a bright flash.

If going christmas tree wasn't enough to show the gomers where we were, the light trail from the rocket did the trick. The triple-A opened up on us with bright orange tracers. Boss jinked the aircraft out of the way.

“Looks like a quad-23,” Boss said, then he transmitted, “Magpie, do you have that triple-A? Cleared in hot.”

In his Australian accent, Magpie lead responded, “Got it, Covey, I'm in from the north. Number two will come in from the north also.”

“Roger. Make your break to the west. I'll be holding off to the east.” Boss swung the airplane around to a north heading, and he watched the target area out of his left window.

“Uh, Boss,” I suggested, “don't you think we should turn off the lights now?” I was really getting uneasy being lit up like, well, Christmas.

“If I turn off our lights, the gunner will probably start firing at Magpie when he pulls off target. I want him to shoot at us, so Magpie will be able to get a bead on him.”

I was really starting to wonder what I had signed up for.

The gunner opened up on us again just as Magpie rolled in, and again we jinked out of the way. Magpie's bombs were really close to the target. Maybe 20 meters short.

“Magpie two, put your bombs 20 meters south of lead's bombs. You're cleared in hot.”

It was hard for me to keep track of where everyone was, since Magpie flight was blacked out. Right after he dropped his bombs, Magpie two called, “Two's off.”

At the same time, the gun started firing at Magpie Two. Then, almost instantly, it was engulfed in Magpie Two's bombs.

“Shit hot,” Boss transmitted. “Do you guys have any more ordnance?”

“Sorry, Covey, that's all we have.”

“Okay, you're cleared to RTB. I had you on target at 35, off at 45. BDA one 23 mike mike destroyed. Unknown KBA. Great job, guys.”

We did some more VR, then headed back to DaNang.

“I guess you noticed how much ground fire and triple-A you can see at night.”

I nodded.

“Well, don't forget, they're shooting at you in the daytime also. You just can't see it as well. That's why I like flying at night. When you can see the triple-A, it's not all that hard to jink out of the way. Kind of like not getting hit when you play dodge ball.”

I swallowed hard. I had never been very good at dodge ball.

27

March 1, 1969

I was scheduled to fly a day mission, but needed to attend a squadron meeting in the morning. Most of the guys in the squadron were in attendance, other than the night fliers and the guys who were out on missions.

The squadron had a rather large briefing room that was occasionally used for mass briefings. A young Lieutenant was standing at the front of the room, waiting to speak to us. He was wearing fatigues, rather than a flight suit, and didn't have any wings on his uniform, so he was obviously a ground-pounder.

There appeared to be a tree growing out of the floor at the front of the room. That got all of our attention.

"Gentlemen," the Lieutenant began, "it's eight o'clock, so let's get started. My name is Lieutenant Waller, from Operation Task Force Alpha."

"TFA," he continued, "is the operation to track enemy movements along the trail. This," he motioned to the tree, "is actually an artificial tree with acoustic and seismic sensors. We plant these along the trail by dropping them from F-4s from Ubon, and then we interrogate them from EC-121s flying along the Thai border."

I looked carefully at the artificial tree, and it sure looked real.

Lieutenant Waller brought out a large map, maybe three by four feet, mounted on a cardboard backing. It had a plot of the Ho Chi Minh Trail.

"We have these sensors along most of the trail now, and can give you real-time information on truck activity. We can receive their movements from the seismic sensors, and we have linguists listening to the acoustic microphones. When we have a lot of trucks moving toward a delta point, like here," he pointed to Delta 43, "and not continuing on to the south, we know there's a truck park or trans-shipment point close by. We'll pass that information on to your Intel folks, and you'll know where to direct your attention."

"Yeah," Speedbrake whispered to me, "I really want to direct my attention to Delta 43."

After the briefing, we all went to the front of the room to examine the tree close up. Even from right next to it, I couldn't tell it wasn't a real tree.

Lieutenant Waller could see I was impressed.

"Nobody can tell they're phony," he said. "We've got some recordings you wouldn't believe. Some of the gomers have had sex with their camp followers right next to our com-mikes and didn't know we were recording them."

I was looking forward to having access to the TFA data. Maybe it would help me get better BDA.

It was time for me to fly a solo day flight. Lieutenant Waller had confided to me that, even though the information had not been officially disseminated to Intel, there really was a lot of activity around Delta 43. He hadn't just been making it up for illustrative purposes.

I decided it was time for me to get a closer look at Delta 43.

I entered the AO and made my way to the vicinity of Delta 43, but kept well off to the east. I flew a racetrack pattern from north to south, and used my gyro binoculars to look for activity in the area.

I just couldn't see anything that looked like a good candidate for a truck park. But, even with gyro stabilized binoculars, it was difficult to see very much from far away. I needed to get closer.

I carefully edged nearer to Delta 43, and everything seemed to be going well. I kept varying my heading and altitude, and started to think that this Delta 43 reputation was a bit overblown. I headed south from Delta 43 to see if I could find anything further down the trail.

Suddenly there was a loud BANG right behind my aircraft, and the plane pitched down violently. I'm not sure which emotion I felt more: fear, or being pissed off at myself for being dumb enough to turn my tail to that gunner and giving him a clear shot at me. That son of a bitch had nailed me.

I pulled back on the yoke and nothing happened. Now I was really getting scared. I tried to bank the aircraft, and the flight controls appeared to operate correctly in roll mode. I was preparing to bail out, since the aircraft was now in a fairly steep dive.

Then I thought, what the fuck, I'll try the elevator trim. It worked! I was able to fly the aircraft using the electric trim. It turned out, the trim cable went out through the right tail boom, and the elevator cables went out through the left boom. Apparently, my elevator cables had been cut by the explosion, but my trim cable was fine. I was still flying. I breathed a sigh of relief.

Just when I thought I had everything under control, the rear engine quit. Now I was in deep shit. The rear engine was the critical engine, and I was only about 4000 feet above the terrain. I jettisoned my rocket pods, feathered the rear prop, headed west toward Saravane, and gave a call on GUARD frequency.

“Mayday, mayday, mayday. Covey 218 has taken a hit. I have flight control problems and lost my rear engine. I'm west of Delta 43, headed toward Lima 44.”

Hillsboro came back on GUARD. That surprised me, since I had assumed they only operated on VHF.

“Roger, Covey 218. We have contacted King and they are scrambling the Jolly Green from NKP. We'll have them head toward Lima 44.”

It was comforting to think that help was on the way, even though there was no assurance at all that I would make it to Lima 44.

As soon as I jettisoned my stores I had slowed to Best Glide Speed, 93 knots. I was not able to maintain altitude, but my sink rate was minimal, perhaps 300 feet per minute. I looked out ahead and could see Lima 44. It was hard to tell if I would make it or not.

I dialed zero mills into my gun sight, and looked at Lima 44 with reference to the pipper. It wasn't moving. It looked like I might just make it. Or maybe come up a little short. And then a funny thing happened.

My asshole started twitching. I had heard about people munching on their seat cushions with their ass, and I'd thought it was just an expression.

“I'll be damned if I ever tell anybody about this,” I muttered to myself.

I kept the landing gear up until I was absolutely sure I would make it to the runway. On short final I put the gear handle down, and the airplane sagged a little as those humongous gear doors opened and created all that drag. Since the hydraulic pump was on the front engine, at least I didn't need to pump the gear down.

I touched down on brick one, and my asshole stopped twitching. I cleared the runway, and there was a nondescript “follow me” vehicle with a Laotian driver waiting to marshal me to a parking spot. I shut down the front engine and exited the airplane. It felt good, really good, to be on the ground.

I looked over the airplane to see how badly it had been damaged. It didn't look too bad. There was a hole from shrapnel in the rear engine cowling, and another hole in the left boom. Other than that, the airplane looked perfectly airworthy. The decision of whether it would fly again was well above my pay grade.

Within five minutes of my arrival, there was an HH-53, Jolly 22, landing alongside my parking spot. I hopped on board and we took off.

I'd never been in a helicopter before. It was a really different experience, with all kinds of unfamiliar vibrations. The pilot in the left seat kept looking back at me and grinning.

It was a short flight to Nakom Phenom Air Base, NKP, sometimes called “naked fanny”.

When we landed, the left seat pilot came back to where I was sitting, and removed his helmet. It was Vince Garner, my room-mate from senior year at the Academy! I hadn't recognized him with his helmet on and his visor down.

"Vince! You're a real life-saver."

"How you been, Ham? Long time no see. There's an extra bed in my hooch. Let's get you settled in and have some mission booze."

"That sounds great to me, but I think I need to contact Covey Ops."

"Yeah, King takes care of all that. They'll get you a phone patch through to DaNang. Come with me."

It was really great to see Vince. This wasn't the first time he had saved my ass. Five years earlier, when we were room-mates during doolie summer, he had made my bed for me in the morning after I had gone to sick bay in the middle of the night. I was still at the Flight Surgeon's office when the room inspections started. When the senior cadet came by to check our room, my bed passed inspection. It was a big deal at the time.

Vince escorted me into the Command Post, and we used a secure phone line to call Covey Ops. Major Walters sounded relieved to hear my voice.

"Hamfist," he said, "I want you to take the rest of the day off at NKP. You could use some time away from DaNang. I'll arrange for a C-130 flight for you tomorrow."

"Thank you, sir."

"You're welcome. One more thing, Hamfist. Have somebody point you to a massage parlor, and get yourself a rub-and-scrub. That's an order."

"Yes, sir."

28

March 1, 1969

It was really great to see Vince and catch up with him. We went to his hooch, and he found me a bed and a place to put my flying gear. Then we headed to the NKP O'Club.

"You're not going to believe how many classmates we have here," he said. "Dave Marshall and Dick Fisher are both flying Spads out of here, and I work with them all the time on SARs. We'll meet up with them at the club."

Going to the NKP O'Club was like old home week. I recognized several guys from my past life, either jocks who were in classes ahead of me at Laughlin, or some guys from some of the senior classes at the Academy.

We ran into Dave and Dick at the Club, just as Vince had predicted. It was really neat to get together with three classmates and catch up with what was happening in our lives since graduation. Dick and Dave had both gotten married right after graduation.

In fact, I had attended Dick's wedding, held at the Academy Chapel the afternoon of

Graduation Day. Cadets weren't allowed to be married, and it was a sort of tradition that many of the guys who were engaged would get married immediately after graduation. In fact, the Academy Chapel was pretty much booked up for the entire day well before Graduation. I was one of the graduates who had held a saber to form a "saber tunnel" for Dick and his bride, Sally, to walk through.

"Check this out," Dick said excitedly, "I'm a dad!" He showed me a photograph of Sally holding a beautiful baby girl.

"She's gorgeous," I said, and I meant it. Some babies look like shriveled old men. This little girl looked like she could be in a Gerber's commercial.

"She was born two days after I arrived at NKP. I haven't even held her yet. I'm going to see her for the first time when we meet up in Honolulu for R&R."

We sat around the bar in the club for a few hours, catching up. It turned out Vince, Dick and Dave were all in the same squadron, the SAR squadron at NKP. Since the Jolly Greens flew so slow and had very little armament, they needed air support.

That's where the Spads came in. The A-1 Skyraider, better known as the Spad, was an antique airplane that had been the workhorse of the Korean War. It was a propeller-driven, heavily-armed attack airplane that carried a great bomb load and had lots of loiter time. Perfect for escorting the Jolly Green.

Vince, Dave and Dick had already worked several high-profile SARs together, and were well on their way to being highly decorated, just like we all used to fantasize about when we were cadets.

We went to dinner together at a small Thai restaurant off base, and then I asked for directions to the nearest, and best, massage parlor.

“I'll go there with you,” Vince said. “Gotta make sure you get back to base in one piece.”

Major Walters had been right. After the stress of the day, a rub-and-scrub was exactly what I needed.

29

March 2, 1969

I caught a flight on a C-130 back to DaNang, and went in to see Major Walters.

“Are you feeling okay to fly again?” he asked.

“Of course. I made a stupid mistake and turned my back on Delta 43. I won't do that again. I'm sorry I lost an airplane.”

“It's not really a loss. I asked one of the FACs from the Nail squadron at NKP to take a mechanic with him to Lima 44 and look at the bird, and it's really minor damage. The control cables in the left boom need to be replaced, and a fuel line to the rear engine was severed. It'll be good as new in a week, and we'll have a Nail pick the airplane up and bring it over here. As for you, I'd like you to get right back on the horse that threw you. If you're up to it, I have you on the 0300 departure tonight.”

“Sounds good to me, sir.”

I went back to my hooch and took a nap, and woke up in time to have a nice meal at the Doom Club before my flight.

My FAN was Pops Carter. Pops was a very senior Major, and was going to retire after this assignment. He had flown as a Navigator on B-25s during World War II, and had a ton of experience. He was the perfect FAN for my first flight after pretty much getting shot down. At first I felt a bit awkward being in command and directing the activities of someone a lot senior to me. But the Air Force regulations clearly stated that the pilot in command is in charge, and I was the pilot in command. And, I'll admit, I got used to it pretty quickly.

We had a fairly routine mission. The only real excitement that we had was when we went to drop a parachute flare.

For some reason, probably corrosion, the arming wire didn't fully pull out of the flare when we released it. After it left the pylon, it hung there in the slipstream, dangling by the arming wire.

Then, as we watched, the arming wire pulled out a little bit, and the flare started sparking. The arming wire had pulled out enough to arm the flare, but it hadn't pulled out enough for the flare to drop. In another thirty seconds, we would have a flare, burning at who knows how many thousand degrees, hanging right under our wing, which was still full of fuel. We were in deep shit.

Instinctively, I tried rocking the wings left then right. No luck. Then it occurred to me that all I needed to do was generate some G-loading on the airplane, to make the flare heavy enough to pull out of the arming wire. I dove the airplane for a few seconds to pick up speed, then pulled up sharply, generating three or four G's. The flare dropped away just a few seconds before igniting.

We conducted night VR along the trail, and really didn't come up with any targets worth attacking. I stayed well away from Delta 43.

While we were in the AO, we could hear a SAR being conducted on GUARD frequency. It was Jolly 22, and it sounded like he was getting heavy enemy reaction.

All I could think was, shit, Vince, get the hell out of there! What the hell were you doing conducting a SAR at night, anyway?

And then all hell broke loose on GUARD. Spad 1 and 2, Jolly 22's escorts, were getting the shit shot out of them. And then I heard them both go down, within two minutes of each other. And then GUARD went silent.

30

March 3, 1969

Vince had told me that he worked exclusively with Dick and Dave. That meant it was Dick and Dave who had gotten shot down last night.

I couldn't believe it. I'd just been drinking with them the night before. Dick had shown me a photo of his family. It wasn't fair. Damn it, it wasn't fair.

After I landed, I went to the Doom Club to get a drink. I really needed somebody to talk to. The past couple of days had been really intense, and now I didn't even have Fish to talk to, because he was on R&R.

I hung around the bar for a while, nursing a scotch and water. I didn't recognize a soul. No shit – anybody with any intelligence isn't drinking at eight o'clock in the morning. And then, in walked Cliff Bowers.

Cliff and I had been on the Academy Gymnastics Team together, and I thought he had gone to grad school after the Academy. But, here he was, in a flight suit.

"Hey, Cliff," I called, "Get your ass over here."

He was as glad to see me as I was to see him. It turned out, he had shown up at the University of Illinois and, as soon as he got there, the Air Force changed his orders and sent him to pilot training.

"Needs of the service," he said.

"I've heard that. So, what're you flying?"

"I'm flying O-2s out of Hue. I brought a bird in for phase check today, and I fly it back tomorrow on a milk run mission. How about you?"

"Me too. I'm flying O-2s over the trail. I got shot down two days ago." Even though I wasn't *really* shot down, it sounded more impressive. Or maybe more stupid.

We spent the rest of the day catching up and swapping war stories.

Then I told him about what I heard on GUARD frequency the night before. I was pretty sure it was Dick and Dave. It bothered the hell out of me.

"We've had a bunch of guys get shot down from my unit in Hue. Good guys," he said. "I'll tell you how I handle it. I just pretend they DEROSed. You know, one-twelfth of our unit DEROSes every month, and we just don't see them anymore. So when a friend gets shot down, I pretend to myself that he simply DEROSed. It works. Sort of works."

“Maybe I'll give that a try.”

Cliff hadn't checked in at the VOQ yet, and I told him about having an extra bed in my hooch. I was sure Fish wouldn't mind. Cliff camped out in my room that night and we stayed up well past midnight shooting the shit.

The next morning, we went to the Doom Club for breakfast, and then he left to fly his bird back to Hue. It was really great spending time with him, and I told him I would try to get a mission, maybe a local Instrument ride, up to Hue real soon.

Before noon, Cliff was dead.

31

March 3, 1969

Cliff and another classmate from the Academy, Jim Fellows, were both shot down within an hour of each other, both flying O-2s. Their bodies were recovered within hours. Jim wasn't a Covey, but he was a Bully FAC, in our sister squadron. We had hung around with each other quite a bit, after I bumped into him at the BX early in my tour.

It was starting to dawn on me that all of my classmates who ended up getting killed had one thing in common: they had all recently come into contact with me. It became clear to me that I was some kind of Typhoid Mary. Not getting killed myself, but causing those I came into contact with to die.

This had to stop. There was only one to do that. I had to become a hermit. I'd be damned if I'd be the cause of any more of my friends dying. I resolved, then and there, to keep to myself and not get close to anyone from my past.

And I would use Cliff's method of dealing with deaths of my friends. I would carry out this mental charade, and pretend that the guy didn't die, he simply DEROSed back to the world.

I kept my fingers crossed every time one of my friends flew a mission, especially a final, “champagne”, flight.

Speedbrake was scheduled to have his champagne flight, and I was worried. We were all gathered on the ramp, waiting for his arrival, with a bottle of champagne and a fire truck waiting to hose him down after he deplaned. And it was well past his arrival time. I felt sick, a physical pain in the pit of my stomach.

Finally, at least twenty minutes late, he landed, taxied in to the parking area, and got hosed down. After the hose-down, we all went to the bar, and Speedbrake bought drinks for the house.

I was going to miss Speedbrake, but I was sure glad to see him go home in one piece.

One of the guys from our squadron had finished his one-year tour of duty well before I arrived, but he was still in our hooch. I had never run into him until today. I bumped into him in the hallway after returning from the bar.

“Hi,” he said, as he offered his hand. “I'm Buzz Watson.”

“I'm Hamfist Hancock,” I returned his handshake.

He smiled. “Hamfist. Interesting.”

"I finished my Covey tour a few months ago," Buzz commented, "and now I'm assigned to a special unit here at DaNang. I leave in a few days for a Forward Operating Location in Laos."

"What are you going to be doing in Laos?" I asked in amazement.

"I was selected for the Steve Canyon Program."

"What's that?" I asked. I'd heard the term before, but no one had really talked about it.

"Well," he answered, "I'll be based out of Vientiane, but doing most of my flying out of FOLs. Doing pretty much what I did as a Covey, but I'll be flying O-1s and T-28s, and I'll have a Laotian observer with me most of the time. I'll be flying in civvies, using the call-sign Raven. And, get this, I'll be getting TDY non-availability every day. Twenty-five bucks a day. Really good deal."

"Sounds pretty cool, but it could get dangerous," I commented.

He reached into the pocket on the left arm of his flight suit and withdrew a pack of Camels. He took a long, hard look at me, lit a cigarette and took a deep drag. "You know, danger is all relative. I don't know if you knew Moss Mossberg."

I shook my head.

"He was a good guy," he continued, "but you wouldn't want to fly with him. A real magnet-ass. Got the shit shot out of himself every mission. Always came back with lots of holes in his airplane. But he never went down, came back every flight. We had a hell of a going-away party for him. He was headed back to the world to get married to his college sweetheart. About a week after he got back, he was walking across the street in L.A., to see a goddam wedding planner, and got wiped out by some asshole drunk driver."

"Can you picture that?" he asked, "Crossing fucking Melrose Avenue and getting killed, after making it through twelve months over Steel Tiger. So tell me, Hamfist, what's more dangerous – Steel Tiger or Melrose Avenue? I'll bet you a month's pay more people get killed every year on Melrose Avenue than over Steel Tiger. So, what I'm saying is, when your number's up, your number's up. If I'm going to die, I'd just as soon have it happen when I'm doing something I love, something that begins with the letter F. And I'm not really into fishing. In the Raven program I'm going to get six more months of great, balls-to-the wall flying. And I'm going to make extra money to boot."

He had a point. For us Lieutenants, getting more flying was almost as good as getting more pay. And this guy, Buzz, was going to be getting $25 a day of non-availability pay.

"By the way," he remarked, as he entered his room, "the best whorehouse in all of Southeast Asia is in Vientiane."

32

March 5, 1969

Fish came back from R&R and looked really good. He didn't have that thousand-yard stare any more, the look that distinguished guys who had been there too long.

“How was R&R?” I asked.

“Fucking awesome. I went to Sydney, and the girls were incredible. It was so great to see some good-looking round-eyes who know how to speak English, even though they talk a little funny. And the food was great. You really need to go to Australia.”

“By the way,” he continued, “I was so tired when I got there, I passed out when I was walking down the sidewalk my first night. I woke up in a hospital bed, and there was an Aussie doctor taking my vital signs. I said to him, 'Hey, doc. Was I brought here to die?' And he says to me,” at that point Fish was laughing so hard it was difficult to understand him, “‘No, mite, you was brought here yestadie'. Get it?” He laughed some more.

I laughed politely, but, honestly, my sense of humor had faded after what I'd been through the past week. But it was sure nice to have Fish back.

"Hey, Fish," I asked, "what's the deal with Buzz? He said he finished his tour a while ago and he's still here."

"Oh, that sonofabitch is crazy! He's on loan to the Rangers to do some special ops stuff, then he's going off to be a Raven. Did he tell you he carries a grease gun with him when he flies?"

"A what?"

"A grease gun – you know, a .45 caliber machine gun. He also carries a model 1911 pistol, and a metal ammo can with 500 rounds. Says he can use the ammo for either gun. He's planning on carrying out a pitched battle if he ever gets shot down."

"Where did he get that kind of hardware?" I asked.

"Oh, he went to the Freedom Hill BX and bought a couple bottles of Johnny Walker and bartered with some marines. You know, the marines can't buy liquor at the BX. So they trade stuff for booze. They write off the weapons as a combat loss, and then they get new stuff."

"How did he get the name Buzz?" I asked, "Did he buzz the tower or something?"

“No,” Fish answered, “Did you see The War Lover, that Steve McQueen movie a few years ago?”

I nodded.

“Well, the Steve McQueen character in the movie, the guy who was the war lover, was named Buzz something. It seemed to fit for Watson the minute he showed up at the squadron. If there was ever a war lover over here it's Buzz.”

33

April 27, 1969

I was asleep at 0800 when I was awakened by a loud explosion and what felt like someone hitting me in the chest. I thought the base was under attack, and I rolled out of bed onto the floor. I landed on broken glass.

The fluorescent light fixture in the ceiling had come down, and there was broken glass everywhere.

There was another, even louder, explosion, and then the base siren started sounding. Again, I felt like someone had hit me in the chest, and I realized that it was the over-pressure from the concussion of the blast. I figured these rockets must be really close.

But they weren't rockets, and the explosions continued. For a long, long time. After a few minutes, I could hear people milling out in the hallway, so I got up and went out of my room.

"What the fuck is going on?" I asked no one in particular.

Balls emerged from his room, carrying his camera, and ran to the exit. "The ammo dump is blowing up. I gotta get some pictures of this!"

I followed him outside, and saw a huge fireball, perhaps 500 feet high, on the other side of the base. After five or six seconds, we heard the explosion and felt the concussion. I ran back to my room and grabbed my camera.

I ran around to the ladder on the north side of the hooch, climbed up onto the roof, and joined the thirty-odd people already there.

It was a sight to behold. Every minute or so there was a huge explosion. Some of the fireballs probably went up 1000 feet or more. After each fireball, there was a small mushroom cloud, looking just like the pictures from atomic bomb tests I watched on our black-and-white television as a kid. And there were people on every rooftop.

The siren was sounding continuously. It occurred to me that if the gomers were smart, they would launch a rocket attack. We would all probably have assumed it was the explosions from the ammo dump. They could have killed a lot of us that day. I guess their bureaucracy was as bad as ours.

The explosions continued for another 23 hours. The air conditioner got knocked out of our window, and every light bulb on base was broken. At one point, some type of anti-personnel gas that had been stored in the ammo dump was set off, and we all had trouble breathing, and it made our eyes burn. There were smoke goggles and masks at the squadron, but not at the hooch. Fortunately, the wind shifted, and the self-induced gas attack didn't last too long.

The story came out that the whole thing started when some troops had been burning the high grass outside the Marine ammo dump, to make sure no sappers could sneak up without being seen. Well, apparently there was a 2.75-inch rocket in the grass. Nobody knew how it got there, but it cooked off and went right into the mouth of the ammo dump, setting off a chain reaction of explosions of historical proportions.

The concussions were so bad that they set off the bombs in the Air Force ammo dump, several miles away, on our side of the base. The shanty town off the north end of the runways was flattened, and the Freedom Hill BX was so badly damaged that it stayed closed for over a month. The sky-cops were stationed in a perimeter around the BX to shoot any looters that tried to take advantage of the situation.

Finally, it was over. All of our missions had been cancelled, of course, and when we ultimately resumed flying, several days later, we only carried four rockets per plane. I thought we had it bad, until I worked a target with a flight of four Gunfighters the next week. Each F-4 was carrying one Mark 81 bomb.

The Mark 81 was a small bomb. Some people called them lady-fingers, like the thin cookies. They were half the size and weight of the standard 500-pound Mark 82.

When I got back from my mission, I asked Major Walters why the Gunfighters didn't just send one F-4 with four bombs, instead of four F-4s with one bomb each.

“Gotta keep up the sortie rate,” he said. “McNamara wants a sortie rate.”

34

May 22, 1969

I was really looking forward to meeting up with Emily in Honolulu for R&R. I had already been eligible several months earlier. The rules were that a pilot had to be in-country at least four months before taking R&R. So I could have gone earlier, but Emily had arranged for vacation in June, so that's what I requested.

R&R was an official military program. It was either five or seven days, depending on the location. Air transportation to the R&R location was provided, but R&R expenses were not. There were a lot of selections: Honolulu, Sydney, Bangkok, Hong Kong, Kuala Lampur, Manila, Tokyo, Singapore and Taipei. Although R&R stood for Rest and Recreation, some pilots referred to it as I&I – Intoxication and Intercourse.

I went to the MARS station to see if I could get a call through to Emily. I wanted to make sure she had plane tickets and to tell her I had reserved a nice room in the Hale Koa, the new military hotel right on Waikiki Beach. We were going to have a great time. And I had a nice surprise to spring on Emily.

When I called her at the D.O.'s office, another receptionist answered, and said that Emily was not available. Strangely, she didn't have any information about when she would be back. I tried her home phone, but there was no answer. I was getting concerned.

I made an appointment at the MARS station to place another call in a few more hours, picked up my mail, and went back to my room.

I had a letter from Emily, and there was something different about it. At first, I couldn't put my finger on it, and then it hit me.

She almost always had a faint imprint of her lipstick, and the annotation "SWAK" on the flap side of the envelope. Although I hadn't asked her to do it, I had become accustomed to each of her letters being Sealed With A Kiss. This one wasn't.

I had a really bad feeling as I opened the envelope.

"Dear Hamilton -

You probably think it's unfair of me to tell you this in a letter, but I think it would be unfair to keep it from you once I've made a decision.

I've loved you since the first time we met. And I think I still love you, but now it's different. I'll admit, I'm not as strong as you. I can't take the constant worrying about you, not knowing if or when you'll ever come home. You said the mission of the Air Force is to fly and fight. Maybe that's what you want, but it's not what I want.

I want a stable life, with someone who puts me ahead of his job. Someone who will be home every night. Someone I won't have to worry about all the time. I met someone like that, and I think you'd like him if you met him under different circumstances.

He's a Lieutenant, like you, but he's a Personnel Officer. We're going to get married in two more months.

I discussed this with Colonel Ryan, and he said I'm making a big mistake. So I felt it would be best if I got a different position on base.

Please don't try to call me and talk me out of this. It's not you, it's me. I'm sorry I'm so weak. I guess I wouldn't have made a good fighter pilot's wife after all.

I hope you understand. I still pray for you every night.

Emily"

I felt totally drained and empty inside. I hadn't realized there were tears streaming down my face as I read the letter. My whole world was falling apart

I slid open the top drawer of my desk and looked at the small velvet box I had placed there two days earlier. I opened it and looked at the diamond ring I had planned to put on

Emily's finger when we were together again in Hawaii. I had special-ordered the ring at the BX, because they normally didn't carry 2-carat diamond rings.

And then I started laughing. It hit me - I could have gotten a bigger diamond, at cost, from Tom! What could I have been thinking, ordering it from the BX? Well, at least now I could return it without being humiliated in front of a friend.

And, Tom really was a friend. He'd been writing to me more than once a week, and genuinely wanted for me to somehow make it to Tokyo. Okay, Tom, that's what I'm going to do.

I walked down to the squadron and cancelled my R&R request for Honolulu. I instead requested Tokyo, and requested a later date, in August.

As my last item of business at the squadron, I completed my volunteer form for the Steve Canyon Program, which contained an automatic six-month tour extension, and submitted it to the Admin clerk.

Then I went back to the hooch and looked for someone to get drunk with. I couldn't find anyone who was awake, so I went to the O'Club, and walked into the DOOM Club bar, wearing my flight cap.

There were three ways a pilot could get hit with a big bar bill at the Club, even with drinks as cheap as they were at the DOOM Club.

One way was to walk into the bar wearing a hat. Another way was to ring the bell that hung over the bar. It was traditional that a pilot would ring the bell after his last flight, right before his DEROS.

The third way was to walk into the bar and yell “Dead Bug”. As soon as anyone yelled that, everyone would immediately lie down on their backs on the floor, waving their hands and legs in the air, like a bug that was dying. The last guy to make it to the Dead Bug position had to buy a round of drinks for everyone in the bar.

I walked up to the bell hanging over the bar, wearing my hat, pulled the chain to ring the bell, and yelled, “Dead bug!”. Everyone looked my way and scrambled to get on their backs, as I stood there. This was going to cost me a small fortune. I didn't give a shit.

35

May 23, 1969

There are many types of drunks. Some are happy drunks, who tell jokes and laugh a lot. Some are nasty drunks, who try to start fights with anyone and everyone. Some are sad drunks, who sit around and cry. Some are quiet drunks, who just sit around and vegetate.

I was told I was a happy drunk. I had to go by what my friends told me, since I had no recollection of the previous day after about thirty minutes at the club.

Apparently, I was also the type of drunk who blacks out. I didn't pass out, I stayed conscious, made conversation, told some great jokes, and was apparently an all-around fun guy. But I had absolutely no recollection of any of it.

I woke up on my bed, still in my flight suit, the next morning. My head was spinning, and my mouth felt like it had cotton in it. I sat up slowly and reached for a bottle of water. It was empty.

I stood up and steadied myself against the wall, and stumbled out into the hallway. I felt like I was choking, and needed to get to the sink in the latrine for some water.

Fish was just coming out of one of the stalls. “Oh, you're finally awake! How're you feeling?”

“Like shit. I need some water, right now.”

“I gotta tell you,” Fish said, “you really know how to throw a pity party. That idea about the chow hall was brilliant.”

“What idea was that?”

“Don't you remember?” he asked.

“Not a thing.”

“Well, you got it in your head around three in the morning that you ought to treat everyone to breakfast. I don't mean everyone at the bar. I mean *everyone*.”

“What did I do?”

“Well, you went to the O'Club cashier and bought a couple rolls of quarters and pennies, then you went to the chow hall and insisted I come along. You handed me the rolls of pennies, and you held onto the rolls of quarters. Every time somebody came in, you took a quarter out of your roll and I took two pennies out of mine, and you treated them to breakfast. Everybody, other than one tight-assed Colonel, thought it was pretty cool. The last thing you did was tell the Colonel to fuck off.”

“Holy shit! I did that?”

"Yeah, but don't worry, he doesn't know who you are." Fish reached into his pocket and pulled out my velcro name tag, which he had thankfully removed from my flight suit at some point or other. "Besides," he said, "the Colonel was a fucking ground-pounder."

I filled my water bottle from the sink and chugged it. Once I got hydrated, I started to feel a lot better. But I sure didn't feel well enough to fly my mission later that night.

I went by my Flight Commander's room and knocked on the door. Major Withers answered and invited me in.

"Sir, I'm really not feeling too well right now. Any chance I can trade flights with someone on a later mission?"

"I beat you to it, Hamfist. When I saw the condition you were in at the Club last night, I figured it was a sure bet you shouldn't be flying tonight. I have you assigned to man the duty desk starting at midnight."

"Thank you, sir."

"Now that you're here, I want to talk to you about that letter you got."

"Oh, you know about it?"

"I think everybody that was at the Club, and probably everybody at DaNang, knows about it. I'm sorry it happened to you, but I'm also glad it happened to you."

"What do you mean, sir?"

“That gal, the one who wrote you the Dear John letter, probably did both of you a big favor.”

I'm sure I looked puzzled.

“Let me tell you about what it was like at Kadena a few years ago,” he continued. “flying F-105s. Kadena was a great base, in Okinawa, the poor man's Hawaii. Life was good. We had great flying, mostly weekends off, and all of us married guys had our families there, since it was an accompanied tour.”

“Sounds pretty nice.”

“It was. Then, one day, out of the blue, we had a no-notice squadron meeting, and we were told we would be leaving for Takhli Air Base, in Thailand, in 12 hours, for an indeterminate time period. Operation Rolling Thunder had just started, and we were going to be part of the initial effort to bomb North Vietnam into submission. I guess you know how that turned out.”

I nodded.

“I went from the squadron to my house on base to tell my wife I would be leaving for combat. I walked into our house and she was giving our daughter a bath. As soon as she saw me, standing there in my flight suit, she knew exactly what was happening. She scooped up my daughter from the bathtub, I think she was about three at the time, and said, 'Charlotte, Daddy has to go away for a little while. Give him a kiss goodbye.' And then she helped me pack."

"My wife is a real fighter pilot's wife," he continued. "She was the squadron commander of our family the whole time I was away. Did everything. Even arranged to have the grass cut."

"Not everybody's wife was like mine. Some of the wives couldn't handle the short-notice call to combat their husbands had received. There were about a dozen wives that had this sick contest, where they would go to the Kadena O'Club every night and see which one could pick up a transient pilot the quickest. They called it their fuck club. They couldn't handle being Air Force wives. Basically, I think they just had nervous breakdowns."

I was starting to get his point. If I had married Emily, she would have been miserable, and that would have made me miserable. And, if we'd had kids, that would have been more lives ruined.

"Thank you, sir. You really helped me put it into perspective."

"Glad I could help, Hamfist."

As I was leaving, Major Withers had one last comment.

"Some of my squadron-mates from Kadena never made it back. They're still up there in North Vietnam, at the Hanoi Hilton."

36

July 22, 1969

One afternoon, when I went to Ops, there was a note waiting for me.

It was from Don Springer, my classmate from pilot training. He'd received an assignment to NKP, in Thailand, and had ferried an OV-10 to DaNang for some maintenance work.

“Hi Ham,” the note read, “I'm at DaNang for a couple of days while I get an airplane fixed. I flew in from NKP this morning. If you want to get together, I'm at the VOQ at Gunfighter Village, room 314. Looking forward to seeing you and hearing some war stories!

Don Springer”

I really liked Don. We'd been in different cadet squadrons at the Academy, but we'd had several classes together and got to know each other pretty well.

I couldn't risk infecting him with the Hamfist curse. I crumpled the note and threw it in the trash.

I still had two weeks to go until my R&R, and I really needed it. I was dog-tired and totally burned out. There were days I just didn't give a shit if I got shot down or not. What the fuck, I thought; when your number's up, your number's up. I found myself taking risks I never would have considered six months earlier.

Like getting in a pissing contest with that 9-level at Delta 43. On this night's mission, we had located a truck park near Delta 43, and it was defended by that quad-23. I called Moonbeam and said I needed fighters, I didn't care what the ordnance load was. Mark 82s, CBUs, even nape, whatever they could send me. They sent me some Navy A-7s from the U.S.S. Kitty Hawk.

I was thrilled. A-7s have a great bombing system, and these navy jocks were among the best. They had the reputation for being able to drive nails with their bombs.

The call sign of this flight was Canyon Passage 21 and 22. They were loaded with Mark 82 slicks. I gave them a radial and distance from Channel 72 for the rendezvous that would put us just north of Delta 43, our target area. They gave me an ETA of 5 minutes, with 15 minutes of playtime.

It was a totally dark, clear night. When the fighters set up an orbit over the rendezvous point, I couldn't see them at all. They were at angels 20, and I was at 9,000 feel. I needed to make sure they could see me and the target area before I marked the target.

"I'm going christmas tree in five seconds," I transmitted. I counted from one-potato to five-potato and turned on all my lights. Beacon, nav lights, landing light, the whole enchilada. I just wanted to get the fighter pilots' eyes in my direction, and then I was going to drop a ground marking flare.

Canyon Passage 21 transmitted, "We have you in sight... Holy shit, Covey, get your fucking lights off!"

The sky around me lit up like the fourth of July. The 9-level gunner had registered on me. Tracers bracketed the left and right side of my fuselage, and I didn't know whether to break right or left. I maneuvered a little, but basically kept flying straight ahead. What the fuck - it's a big sky!

I turned off my lights and confirmed that the fighters had the target area in sight. I gave them the target elevation and wind information.

I instructed the fighters, "Okay, guys, we need to go after the gun first, then we'll hit the truck park. If you still see the target, you're cleared in from north to south, with a right break."

I set up a holding pattern east of the target, and shortly Canyon Passage 21 called, "Lead's in from the north". As soon as he made his radio call, there was withering 23 mike mike fire in the direction of north, from the target.

"Break it off, lead," I called, "we have a gomer tuned in." It was obvious this guy was listening in on our strike frequency. "I want you to make your next pass from Seattle to Miami, with a break toward Mexico City, and when you call in I'll go christmas tree again."

My FAN, Tightass Tilton, was really not too keen to do this. He was probably the only guy in the squadron whose name actually suited him. He was constantly uptight. Every time I flew with him, he would whine that he wanted to go higher, stay further away from the target, RTB sooner. He especially didn't want to go near Delta 43. He was a young guy, a bachelor like me, right out of Nav school. If he had been a married guy, with a family, I could have understood his reluctance to get in a good fight. As it was, I just considered him a pussy.

"Uh, Hamfist," he protested, "I don't think that's a good idea."

"It'll be fine," I lied, "I'm just going to turn the lights on for a second, then I'll break hard out of the way."

Tightass squirmed.

Lead called in from Seattle, and I turned on all the lights again. One potato, two potato, lights off, just as our friend the 9-level gunner opened up on us with all barrels. I broke hard to the left as tracers whizzed by the right side of the aircraft. One out of every four rounds was a tracer, and it looked like a solid line of light. Through the open right window we could hear the staccato clicking of the rounds as they went by, followed, a few seconds later, by the actual sound of the gun firing. The smell of cordite filled the cockpit.

The triple-A on the ground from the 9-level was in mid-fire when it was engulfed by the massive explosion of lead's bombs. Lead had chosen, wisely, to expend all of his ordnance on that one pass, while he had the gunner in his sights. For some reason, secondary explosions started cooking off about 20 meters away, to the south.

This was great. I had destroyed my nemesis, the Delta 43 gunner, and I didn't need to use ground marking flares to direct number two to the truck park. I simply referenced the two sets of explosions on the ground. “Number two, we have two sets of fires 20 meters apart, oriented north to south. I want you to put all your bombs 50 meters east of the northern fire. I want you to run in from Chicago to Denver and break to San Francisco. One pass, haul ass.”

Number two dutifully came in from the northeast and pulled off to the right. There was no anti-aircraft fire at all. We were rewarded with huge secondary explosions, right on the truck park! The fires were so bright they blanked out the starlight scope. With the naked eye I could see at least fifteen trucks burning. Now *that* is what I called BDA!

Canyon Passage 21 flight was winchester, and we were bingo, so it was time to RTB. Tightass didn't say a word the entire flight back. I figured he was as pumped as I was.

After landing, Tightass headed straight to the Ops Officer's office and slammed the door. I went to the Intel room and gave a thorough debriefing. Just as I was finishing, Major Walters came in. "Hamfist, can I see you for a minute?" I joined him in his office and closed the door.

"Lieutenant Tilton said he doesn't want to fly with you anymore," he commented, "He said you act like you have a death wish."

"No, sir," I bristled, "actually I have a desire to do my job. And tonight, I'd say I really did it." I found myself raising my voice, "I destroyed the most deadly triple-A piece in all of Steel Tiger, and I think I got the best BDA this squadron's seen in months."

"Lieutenant," he came back – I knew I was probably in trouble when he didn't call me Hamfist – "that's commendable, but there isn't a target in all of Steel Tiger that's worth your life or another one of my airplanes. You weren't on a SAR, you didn't have TIC, it was just a goddam truck park. You probably wiped out a dozen gomers. And that quad-23. Good for you. Tomorrow Uncle Ho will send down a dozen more, along with a new gunner. You're taking stupid risks, and I won't have it. Pack your bags, Lieutenant. You're out of here!"

I was shocked. “What!” I yelled, “Sir! You're kicking me out of the squadron?”

“No such luck, Hamfist,” he answered, “you're leaving for R&R tomorrow.”

37

July 23, 1969

The Ops Officer, Major Walters, had made a wise decision to send me on R&R immediately. If I had been allowed to continue flying combat for another two weeks until my scheduled departure, there was no telling if I ever would have lasted.

I had gotten what the fighter jocks called "target fixation", where they would be on a bombing run and trying so hard to meet their parameters for a good delivery, they would lose awareness of their altitude and end up auguring in.

I had seen that first-hand a few weeks earlier, and the horrific sight will forever burned into my memory. I was controlling a flight of two F-4s from DaNang, Gunfighter 55 and 56, on a truck park one night. It was a low-threat area, and I wasn't all that concerned about enemy reaction. I had gone christmas tree for an extended period of time, and hardly even drew any small arms fire. This was going to be easy.

Gunfighter 55 put his bombs right on target, and we got a few small secondaries. Then Gunfighter 56 rolled in. Shortly after he called rolling in, there was a terrific fireball, right on the target. I figured his bombs must have hit something really lucrative, to get that big a secondary.

"That's beautiful," I transmitted.

Lead came back, "Negative, Covey. That was my wingman."

The guy had flown right into the ground. We stuck around the area for over an hour, to see if maybe he had punched out and would come up on the radio. No such luck.

I did a lot of soul-searching, to see if there was anything I could have done to have prevented the tragedy. No, I gave a good target briefing, I provided the correct target elevation, I gave a good mark and a good run-in line. The guy had probably simply gotten target fixation. It can happen to the best of pilots.

The last thing I did before I got on the "freedom bird" to Tokyo was change my MPC into U.S. Dollars. We weren't allowed to have U.S. Currency in Vietnam because, they said, it could lead to black marketeering. So all U.S. Forces were paid in Military Payment Certificates. Basically monopoly money.

Periodically, everyone would have to turn in their MPC to exchange it for new, different, MPC. This supposedly kept MPC out of the hands of the locals, since they never knew when the money would be changed. To be honest, I never really totally understood the whole MPC thing. But finally I was getting my hands on good old greenbacks.

It was a late night departure, and I slept the entire flight, probably five or six hours. I arrived at Yokota Air Base at 0700 hours. I wasn't sure if I should call Tom so early, but he said to call him any time. I found a pay phone in the terminal, and dialed the number on his *meishi*. A female with an accent answered.

"All American Import Export. Mr. Marcos's office."

"Hi, this is Hamfi...uh, Hamilton Hancock calling for Mr. Marcos." I'd almost called myself Hamfist.

After a short pause, Tom was on the phone. "Ham! Great to hear from you. When are you coming to Tokyo?"

"Hi Tom. Actually, I'm already here. I'm at Yokota Air Base."

"Yokota Air Base..." he repeated, "Okay..." He paused, "It will take my driver about an hour to get there. He'll meet you at the main gate in an hour. Is that okay?"

"Sure, great. How will I know your driver?"

"He'll have a sign with your name. Damn, I'm really glad you're here! And your timing is perfect. If you had come two days earlier, you would have missed us. We just came back from Boston. I'll see you soon."

I was actually glad to have an hour to decompress. Yokota Air Base was like being back in the States. They had a great BX right in the terminal, there was a snack bar that actually had *lemons* in the ice tea, and, most important, nobody was lobbing rockets at us. I checked at the Information booth to find out how to get to the main gate, and they pointed me to a line of taxis right outside the door. Now *this* was civilization!

I showed up at the main gate, and there was a blacked-out limo parked at the curb. A young Japanese man was holding a sign with my name. "welcome to Japan," he intoned, with a rather thick accent. "First, we measure."

From seemingly out of nowhere an older Japanese gentleman, in a suit, appeared, and started taking my measurements. He must have measured me fifty different ways, my neck my chest, my arms, my wrists, my inseam, you name it. He was rapidly speaking to a cute young Japanese girl, who was furiously writing down everything he said. It probably took about five minutes. Then the driver opened the door for me, and we were on our way.

The limo was decidedly different from Tom's limo in San Francisco. The car was obviously Japanese, with the driver sitting on the right. The seats were velour, and the headrests had white cloth doilies covering them. The air conditioning was on.

"Temperature okay? Too hot? Too cold?" the driver inquired.

"It good," I responded, not realizing that I was again using pidgin English.

"You want drink?" he offered.

When I said, "Yes, thank you," he handed me an ice-cold beverage bottle. I looked at it. The label said "Calpis". It kind of looked like cow piss, but I sure wasn't going to insult the driver, so I took a sip. Then another. It tasted great.

Tokyo was a study in contrasts. The city was totally modern – it could have been New York or Chicago. But then I'd see women wearing kimonos, carrying brightly colored paper umbrellas, walking with men wearing business suits. It was hard to believe that this place had been bombed to the ground just twenty-five years earlier. I wondered if Vietnam would recover as quickly once the war was over.

38

Tom was waiting at the curb when we arrived outside his office. I got out of the car and went to shake his hand, but he'd have none of that. He went for the big hug.

“I'm afraid I still smell like Vietnam,” I ventured.

“No problem, we'll take you to my place and you can freshen up. The tailor should be ready for your first fitting after you clean up.”

I really wasn't sure how to respond. We both got back into the limo, and we drove to Tom's apartment.

Tom had a nice townhouse within view of Tokyo Tower. “The American Embassy is not very far,” he offered, pointing toward the tower. “The one thing I'll ask you to do,” he said, as we entered, “is remove your shoes.” Then he paused, “You look like you can use some new shoes. What size are you?”

I looked down at my shoes and was immediately chagrinned. I still had the muck of Vietnam on my soles. Why hadn't I used my hour at Yokota to make myself presentable? "I think I'm a size 10."

"No sweat," he replied, "Same as me. We'll find you something."

It was a really nice apartment. There was a modern living room with a couch and two easy chairs, a kitchen, and three bedrooms. The bedrooms had straw mats covering the entire floor, and the mattresses were directly on the floor.

"These are tatami mats," he explained. "You'll love sleeping on a mattress on the floor. You'll see."

"I'm looking forward to it," I responded. I'd slept in a thicket in the jungle, in a room underneath an artillery range, and in a hooch with the air conditioner being knocked out of the wall. I figured I could sleep on a mattress on the floor.

Tom pointed to a separate room with a translucent sliding door. "You can take a shower here".

"Good," I responded, "I need to use the bathroom."

"Not in there, I hope!" Tom replied. "I think you mean you need to use the toilet. In Japan, the bathroom is where you take a bath or shower, and the toilet is in a different part of the house." Tom showed me to the toilet, and then I went to the bathroom to take a shower. Now *that* would take some getting used to!

The shower was different from anything I had seen in the States. As soon as I selected hot water, a gas burner ignited, and the water was instantly hot. When I finished the shower, the burner turned off. There was a white terry cloth robe waiting for me when I finished, and I really felt refreshed. I had been living in the most civilized hooch in Vietnam, but the showers there were nothing compared to this.

When I emerged from the bathroom, the older gentleman who had measured me at the main gate of Yokota was waiting in the living room, holding a dark blue suit. It wasn't really a suit, yet. It was what looked like pieces of a suit, held together with thin white thread.

“We do first fitting now,” he said in a thick accent.

I changed into my underwear, and carefully put on the suit jacket, and he started making miniscule adjustments, moving the material a few millimeters here, a few there, and pinning the material in place. Then I put on the pants and went through the same process. Then I returned the pants to the tailor.

He spoke a few words to Tom in Japanese.

“Do you want single vent or double vent?” Tom asked.

“Single vent”.

“Pleats or no pleats?” Tom continued.

“I really hadn't given it any thought. What do you think?” I responded.

Tom spoke in Japanese again, and the tailor left with the suit. “We're going for no pleats, single vent, single breast, notch lapels. Functional buttons on the sleeves. That's the way you can tell a really good suit,” he said.

“Tom,” I objected, “you really don't need to do this for me. I feel like I'm really putting you out.”

“Don't be ridiculous,” he countered. “I've been waiting for more than six months to show you a good time in Tokyo.” He paused, “And you can't do that unless you're really well dressed. Now let's find you a shirt and tie.”

I put on some civvies, and we got back into Tom's limo. This time, we were going to go to a store in the shopping arcade of the Imperial Hotel.

The hotel was directly across the street from the Imperial Palace. “The Emperor lives there,” Tom motioned in the direction of the palace. “Frank Lloyd Wright designed this hotel,” he said, with an expansive wave of his hand.

We went into the shopping arcade on the lower mezzanine and entered a store that had bolts of cloth in every color imaginable. And every material. Tom looked through several, held one up alongside my face, and announced, “This is the one. Off-white Summer French Batiste.” He spoke to the proprietor, again in Japanese, and again I was measured. Then he picked out several ties that, I figured, would go well with the suit and shirt.

Just as we got in back in the limo, Tom apparently remembered something. He rattled off some more Japanese to Yuji, the driver, and Yuji went running back into the hotel. A few minutes later, he emerged with a small box.

39

July 23, 1969

We were back at Tom's apartment.

"Tom," I said, "I really feel awful taking you away from your job on such short notice."

"Don't be ridiculous," he countered. I'm the boss. I can take off whenever I want."

Tom looked at his watch, then called to Yuji, who had been waiting by the front door. "*Yuji-san. Onaka-ga sukimashita. Ikimasho.*

Yuji made a motion halfway between a head nod and a bow. "*Hai, dozo.*"

And with that, we went back into the limo.

"Have you ever had sushi?" Tom asked.

"I don't think so," I responded, "I had chop suey once."

Tom ignored my *faux pas* and said, "I think you'll like it. It's a pretty standard casual Japanese meal."

We pulled up outside a plain shop with a cloth curtain hanging in the doorway.

"This way," Tom said.

Inside was a "U" shaped counter, ringed with bar stools. Raised about a foot above the counter was a conveyor belt, a dead-ringer miniature of the conveyor belts used for luggage at airports. On the conveyor were small dishes with various small snacks, usually rice wrapped in seaweed. There were at least a dozen different variations. As the conveyer moved, the dishes made their way down the counter.

Tom motioned to a bar stool and said, "Have a seat," then he pulled up a stool next to me and sat down.

"Here's the deal," he explained, "When you see something you like, you just take it off the conveyor and put it in front of you. When you finish eating, you stack up your dishes."

Tom reached into a box on the counter and removed two sets of chopsticks, wrapped in paper. He also grabbed two tea bags and two cups. He put the tea bags in the cups and turned a small faucet that discharged hot water.

"Now," he said, "I'm going to teach you how to act Japanese."

For the next hour he guided me on how to use chopsticks, how to determine which sushi dish had *sashimi* – raw fish – and which had more mundane fare, and how to slurp tea. We had a great time.

After lunch, we went back to Tom's apartment. "Look," he said, "I have just a few loose ends to clean up at the office, and you look like you could use a nap. I'll be back about six, and Miyako should be back from Haneda by then, and we'll all go out. Your suit and shirt will be ready before that."

I didn't object. To be honest, I was dead tired. I went to the bedroom, closed the room-darkening shades, and was asleep within minutes.

In what seemed like no time, it was time to get up.

"Ham," Tom was softly calling to me, trying not to wake me too suddenly, "you ready to go to town?"

"I sure am," I said. I felt totally refreshed. And for the first time in over six months, I felt really clean. The mattress on the *tatami* mats had been incredibly comfortable, and my concerns about it perhaps hurting my back had been totally unfounded.

When I entered the living room, the tailor was once again waiting, holding a now-completed suit. But he wasn't going to leave until he was satisfied it fit perfectly. It did.

The suit was absolutely gorgeous. It was a midnight blue, glimmering "sharkskin" appearance, and fit better than anything I've ever worn, including the custom uniforms we had at the Academy. The shirt was waiting on the coffee table, and I unwrapped it and tried it on. Again, perfect.

Tom walked up to me, held up the ties he'd bought earlier in the day next to my suit, and pronounced, “This is the one.”

Then he handed me the small box the driver had retrieved earlier. I opened it and saw two cufflinks with absolutely perfect, matched, pearls.

“Tom,” I objected, “I just can't let you do all this for me.”

“Ham,” he answered, “you only come to Tokyo for the first time in your life once. I want it to be special.”

Just then, the apartment door opened.

I heard a soft-spoken female voice, “*Tadaima*!”

“Miyako is here, and she brought our lawyer from the airport,” Tom remarked.

A very attractive Japanese lady entered the room, walked right up to me, held out her hand, and bowed slightly. I had expected her to be wearing a kimono, but she was wearing a conservative, grey dress.

She had a slight accent, “I'm Miyako. Thank you for saving my husband's life!” She gripped my hand with both of hers.

“It's a real pleasure to meet you, Miyako. I'm not so sure I saved his life, but I'm glad I was there to help.”

Tom interjected, “Here comes my lawyer.”

A gorgeous Eurasian woman, about my age, entered the room, rushed over to Tom, and hugged him. “Daddy!”

Tom hugged her back, then introduced me, “Samantha, this is the Hamilton I've been telling you about.”

She held out her hand. “Call me Sam.”

I shook her hand, and said, “Sam, it's a real pleasure to meet you. I'm Ham.”

“Sam I'm Ham,” she responded, “sounds like we're reading a Doctor Seuss book.”

Tom beamed. “That's my girl. Sharp as a whip. She finished at the top of her class at Harvard Law School last month. We're so proud of her.”

Sam appeared to blush.

“Now,” Tom said, “let's go have a great dinner. Do you like steak?”

He didn't have to ask me a second time.

While I put on my suit and tied my tie, Tom changed to an equally outstanding outfit. We all got into the car, and Tom said something in Japanese to the driver.

“The absolute best steak in Tokyo is at the Misono Steak House, in Akasaka,” Tom announced.

We drove through narrow streets for about a half hour, and pulled up outside a small restaurant front.

We went into a dimly-lit, elegant restaurant, and sat at a table with a large skillet built into the surface. Tom and Miyako sat on one side of the table, and Sam sat next to me, on my right. I think she purposely positioned herself there to help me with my chopsticks if I had trouble. A chef appeared with four thick steaks, some shrimp, and an assortment of vegetables, and he proceeded to cook them in front of us. He put on an incredible performance, slicing and dicing the steaks and then tossing the pieces of meat over his head and catching them in the rice bowls in front of each of us.

"This is Kobe beef," Tom explained. "Every minute of their lives these animals are massaged, and they're fed beer all day long. The meat is tender enough to cut between your chopsticks. You'll see."

"And, by the way," he continued, "from now on, we're not calling them chopsticks. They're *hashi*."

"Got it. *Hashi*," I answered.

"Ham went to the Air Force Academy," Tom explained, looking at Sam.

"Where'd you go for undergraduate?" I asked Sam.

"I graduated from Northwestern in 1966."

We ate in silence for a few minutes, with me trying my best to impress my hosts, and especially Sam, my facility with *hashi*. I was getting pretty good, getting almost every bite to my mouth without dropping anything.

Then Sam ventured, "You know, I almost dated a cadet once."

"Sounds like you dodged a bullet," I replied.

"No, I was actually really looking forward to it. In the fall of 1963, when I was a sophomore, the Army and Air Force were playing their first-ever football game, at Soldier Field in Chicago."

I remembered it well. I was a doolie at the time, and the entire cadet wing was going to travel to Chicago by train to watch the game and then have a post-game formal ball. We were going to have a joint ball with the "Woops" – the West Pointers – who had also come to Chicago en masse. As a doolie, I had never gotten the opportunity to leave the base since entering the Academy in the summer, and this was going to be a real treat. After the game, we would have about four hours to be out on our own to explore Chicago before the ball. I was really looking forward to it.

Then, the day before our departure, my appendix burst and I had peritonitis. I had emergency surgery, and couldn't go on the trip. I was stuck in the Academy hospital, to watch the game – Air Force beat Army – on television. The only cadet in the hospital. In fact, I was the only patient in the entire hospital, other than a Math instructor's wife, who was only there for about three days to deliver her baby.

"There was a formal ball after the game," Sam continued, "and they wanted local college girls to be blind dates for the cadets. It sounded like it would be fun, and I volunteered. I bought a beautiful gown and gorgeous long, white leather formal gloves. And shoes. Remember?" She looked over at Tom and Miyako. They nodded.

"I showed up at the ball, and I was as dolled-up as I could be. I'd gone to the hairdresser and had my hair done in the morning, and had my nails done also. And the cadets were so handsome in their mess uniforms. Is that what it's called?"

"Mess dress," I answered.

"That's right, mess dress. And I'm not just saying this, Ham, I thought the Air Force cadets looked a lot sharper than the West Pointers."

"It goes without saying," I answered.

"So, I went to the reception hall where all the girls were assembling, and one by one the social director called out the names of the girls and they would go through the door to the ballroom and meet their blind dates." She paused, took a deep breath, and swallowed hard. "And then I was left all alone. I didn't have a date."

"What!" I exclaimed. "Were they crazy?"

"No, it was just, the blind dates had already been pre-arranged, and the cadet I was supposed to be paired up with was in the hospital. I went back to my dorm room and cried myself to sleep."

Tom and Miyako were staring at me.

"Ham! Are you all right? You're white as a sheet."

I found myself frozen, with my chopsticks, okay, my *hashi*, half-way to my mouth, and I couldn't move. Finally, I regained my composure.

"That was me! I was the cadet in the hospital!"

Now it was Sam's turn to be speechless.

Tom looked at Miyako and said, "*Sore wa narimasu*". She nodded. Then he looked at me.

"I'm sorry for speaking Japanese, Ham. What I said to Miyako was that when something is meant to be, it will be."

My eyes locked onto Sam's and I remembered: that was exactly what Colonel Ryan had said.

40

July 23, 1969

The meal was absolutely fantastic. The steak was as tender as Tom had described – actually soft enough to cut with my *hashi*. We made small talk the rest of the meal, but I couldn't get it out of my mind how Sam and I were supposed to have met some six years earlier.

Some of my classmates had met their future wives at that ball. They had dated for the next three and a half years, and then married on graduation day. I had attended their crossed-saber weddings at the Academy Chapel. I felt a sense of loss, the missing moments we could have shared together.

Or maybe we wouldn't have. I was certainly not mature enough to handle an adult relationship at the time. I might have totally blown it. And I knew I was definitely a different person now, after my recent combat experiences, than I was just seven months earlier.

After dinner, Tom probably sensed that Sam and I had some unfinished – actually un-started – business.

"Miyako and I are going to head back to the apartment. But it's still early. Sam, why don't you show Ham around Tokyo?"

"Okay, Daddy." There was an eagerness in her voice, and I was really happy to hear it. She looked at me. "Are you a good dancer?"

"They gave us dance lessons at the Academy. I think I can hold my own."

"Great. There are some new clubs that opened up since I was last in Tokyo, and I've been looking forward to checking them out."

We left the restaurant, and Tom and Miyako went to their waiting car. As he left, I saw him hand Sam some Japanese money, called yen, along with his American Express card.

"Have a great time, kids," he said.

It was funny to be called a kid, after what I'd just gone through for the past seven months, but it was kind of comforting at the same time.

Sam hailed a cab and spoke to the driver in Japanese.

"You speak Japanese also?"

"Oh, yes. I was born in Japan, and went to elementary and junior high school here."

"You were born here? So are you a Japanese citizen?" I asked.

"Actually, for the first twenty-two years of my life, I had dual citizenship. Daddy was stationed at Itazuke Air Base right after the war. So I have American citizenship from being born on base, and I have – no, had – Japanese citizenship because Mommy is Japanese. I had to choose what country I wanted to be a citizen of when I was twenty-two."

"And you chose America."

"Yes. It was an easy choice. I have a strong emotional bond to everything Japanese, but there is no country in the world that can even come close to the United States."

"So when did you first go to the United States?"

"I was about two, I think. Daddy left the Air Force and started his business in the Bay area. We lived in Walnut Creek until I was seven. Then we moved to Tokyo."

"Was it difficult to adjust to living in Japan and going to Japanese schools?"

"Not really. I went to a school for *gaijins*, foreigners. But the curriculum was the same as Japanese schools, much more strict than American schools. We had six days of school every week, and only one month off for summer vacation."

"Sounds pretty tough."

"Well, I didn't really know anything different. When we moved back to the States, when I was fifteen, high school was a piece of cake. I ended up taking advanced courses, and got good grades. Really good grades."

"Were you class valedictorian?"

She seemed a bit embarrassed by the question. “Yes, I was.”

“Did you go to Northwestern on a scholarship?”

“We'll talk about me later. We've arrived at Roppongi. This is where the new clubs are.”

We got out of the taxi and walked around. There were bright lights indicating snack bars, coffee shops and restaurants in front of virtually every building. I noticed a lot of the clubs had American names: Club New York, Denver Cafe, and Greenwich Village Place.

“Let's go in here,” she said, pointing to a sign that read, “Stallion Club”.

We went down some dimly-lit stairs, and the strains of American rock and roll music got louder as we descended.

The place was packed, mostly with Japanese, but an occasional *gaijin* guy. The foreigners all looked, from their haircuts, to be military.

We got a table, ordered some drinks, and it was time to dance. Sam put her purse on the table and we went to the dance floor.

“Aren't you worried about somebody walking off with your bag?” I asked.

“We're in Japan. Nobody steals here.”

We danced for hours. They were playing nothing but American rock and roll songs. Sam didn't seem to be embarrassed by my dancing, so I guess I did okay. My only complaint, if I had any, was that there weren't enough slow dances. Sam was a really great dancer, and she had a sensuous way of slow dancing that made me feel like I was the only person in her world.

Before I knew it, it was two o'clock, closing time. The time had passed all too quickly.

“Are you hungry?” she asked.

“Kind of, but I don't think we'll find any place open at this hour, will we?”

“We're in Roppongi. It's a section of Tokyo where there's always something open. There's a great little place just up the street.”

We walked a few blocks to a building that could have passed for an American diner. The sign read, “Hamburger Inn”.

We sat in a booth, facing each other, and ordered some hamburgers and coffee.

“You know, Ham, I had a really good time tonight. You're a good dancer, for an Air Force guy.”

“I think that's a compliment. So, you were going to tell me about your scholarship to Northwestern.”

“I actually had two scholarships. One for academics and one for women's track.”

“Wow. Impressive.”

“I actually felt kind of bad, taking the scholarships, because there were probably a lot of other kids who needed it more.”

“I guess your dad was already pretty well off by then?” As soon as I asked the question, I a felt like an idiot. How could I be so gauche – I knew better than to ask people about their personal financial situations.

She didn't seem to mind. “Yeah, he was already pretty well established, with offices in Japan and the States. But I had my own money.”

“Really?”

“When I was younger, about the time I was eight to twelve, I did a lot of modeling for magazine ads. The Japanese really like *gaijin* kids in their ads, and I made a small fortune. I still have some of the pictures in my scrapbook. I'll show you when we get back to the apartment. Anyway, I saved it all for college. In the end, I knew I wanted to go on past undergrad, so I took the scholarships to Northwestern so I would still have money for law school. How about you, you must have been pretty smart to get into the Academy.”

“Well, I got good grades in high school, but the most important thing to the Academy was my extracurricular activities. I was president of a lot of clubs, and participated in some sports. I even lettered in Wrestling.”

We talked on for hours. Before I knew it, the small talk had ended, and I found myself spilling my guts to Sam. I felt really close to her, and could tell she wouldn't be judgmental, even as I broke down and cried a few times.

I told her about being a Summary Courts Officer for Mitch, about my Dear John letter, about my belief in fatalism, about Delta 43 and the gunner, and, finally, about my fear that coming into contact with me was the kiss of death for my friends.

"So let me get this straight, Ham. You're a fatalist, right? When your number's up, your number's up, right?"

I nodded. "No question. I've seen guys who were desperate to stay alive getting killed, and guys who didn't give a shit, sorry, didn't care, not getting a scratch."

"And you told me about your friends Dick and what's-his-name both getting killed on the same day right after they saw you."

I nodded, "Dave, his name was Dave. And there was Cliff and Jim."

"Ham, you seem like an intelligent guy. So tell me, was Dick's number up? Was Dave's number up? Was Cliff's number up? Was Jim's number up? Because if their numbers were up, it couldn't have been seeing you that caused them to get killed. Right?"

"Oh, my God! You're right!"

I felt like I had been in a dark room and someone had just turned on a light.

41

July 24, 1969

It was almost six o'clock when we arrived back at the apartment. Tom and Miyako were sitting at the kitchen table, having breakfast.

"I guess you kids had a good time," Tom remarked. "And at least Sam's not carrying a Gideon bible."

We all laughed. Not nervous laughter, real laughter. It was adorable the way both Miyako and Sam lifted their hands to cover their mouths when they laughed.

"I'm appointing Sam to be your official tour guide for the next couple of days. Is that okay with you, Ham?" Tom asked.

"Sure," I responded. I didn't want to appear too eager, but I think my voice gave it away.

"I don't know about you," Sam said, "but I'm going to take a nap. Let's plan on going out about two o'clock."

I went to my room and got into bed. All I could think about was the last twelve hours. And, before I knew it, I was asleep.

Then Sam was knocking on my door.

"C'mon, sleepy head. Tokyo awaits! No suit today, wear some casual civvies."

I got dressed, brushed my teeth, and went to the kitchen. Sam was sitting at the table, drinking a cup of coffee. Another cup was waiting for me.

"My guess is you drink your coffee black. Correct?" she asked.

"You guessed right."

I couldn't get over how great she looked. Any girl can look good when she gets all dolled up to go out at night. But to look *that* good first thing in the morning – our morning, anyway – was really impressive.

"Did you bring your camera with you?" she asked.

"I sure did."

"Good. Bring it along. And don't forget your military ID."

We went outside and walked down the street toward Tokyo Tower.

"Let's go up the tower first, while the weather is still nice," she suggested.

"You're the tour guide."

We walked the mile or so to Tokyo Tower, and took the elevator to the top. It was, surprisingly, a very clear day. Sam pointed out the various landmarks. I could see Tokyo Bay off in the distance, and, far away, Mount Fuji in the other direction.

After spending about an hour in the Tower, we left and walked to a subway station.

"The quickest way to get around Tokyo," she said, "is by train. Follow me."

We walked up to a machine with a coin slot, Japanese writing and about a dozen buttons. Sam pointed to the map on the wall, indicated which station we were currently in, and inserted a few coins. She pressed one of the buttons, and two small cardboard tickets were spit out into the small cup at the bottom of the machine.

I followed her as we went through a entry gate, where an attendant punched a hole in the ticket, and then we walked onto a platform.

"You can set your watch by the trains," she said. An electronic sign indicated that a train would be along in one minute. Then forty-five seconds. Then thirty seconds. The train arrived exactly on schedule.

We got on the train. It was packed, and there was an attendant on the platform pushing against the few people who still had body parts in the way of the doors. The doors closed, and we were on our way.

Sam pointed out the map just above the windows of the train, showing the route and the stations. Some of the names were in English and Japanese, some only in Japanese.

We got off the train at the Ginza station and surrendered our tickets to an attendant as we exited to the street. Other than everyone looking Asian, we could have been in New York. Actually, we could have been in Greenwich Village. Or, for that matter, Haight Ashbury. There were a lot of young people with spiked hair, green hair, purple hair, ear rings, nose rings. The same kind of weirdoes I'd seen in San Francisco.

After about an hour, we got back onto the train.

"You brought your ID, right?" Sam asked.

"Sure. I always have it. Why?"

"When I was a kid, I hung around a lot of military brats, and they took me to the Sanno a lot. It's a military officer's club in Akasaka. I haven't been there in years, but I think we'll both like it."

We got off the train at the Akasaka Mitsuke station and walked about a block to the Sanno Military Facility. It was an old, elegant building, and the receptionist asked to see my ID before we could enter.

Once inside, I could see why Sam had liked the place so much. The Sanno was a first class hotel, and had all the accoutrements of a great establishment. Several restaurants, gift shops, a BX, barber shop, the works. And they accepted dollars, not yen.

“It's my turn to treat. Are you hungry?” I asked.

“Actually, I really am. Is it okay if we go to that restaurant?” she asked, pointing to the Italian restaurant.

“Sure.”

“This is famous as one of the best Italian restaurants in all of Tokyo. And that's really saying something.”

She was right. After eating at military chow halls for seven months, I had started to believe that Italian food was the spaghetti or lasagna that passed for authentic fare. But here was real risotto and cannelloni. Sam and I split each entree in half, to allow us to enjoy both dishes. Then we finished off with the most delicious tiramisu I've ever had. It was more than just a meal. It was a trip to Italy.

After dinner, we wandered around the hotel and ended up at the gift shop. Sam lingered at a display, and then picked up a small, round doll. It was unique. It was a funny, fat shape, and it had no eyes.

“This is a *daruma*,” she said. “Watch this.”

She tipped the doll over, and it rolled back upright, because the bottom of the doll was weighted. .

“The saying goes, seven times down, eight times up. Daddy used to call me Daruma when I was a kid.”

“Why was that?”

"Right after we came back to Japan, I had an accident. For a long time, I couldn't walk. I had a lot of setbacks, but eventually, I was able to walk, and then run. As I said, I ended up running track by the time I was in high school."

"That's really impressive."

"I had a lot of faith, a lot of support, and a lot of luck. I prayed a lot. And I didn't give up."

"I noticed the doll doesn't have any eyes. Why is that?" I asked.

"When you receive a *daruma*, you paint an eye on it when you set a goal. When you reach your goal, you paint the other eye on it. When I was a little girl, right after my accident, I received my *daruma*, and I painted one eye on it to represent walking again. A few years later I painted the other eye. I'll show you when we get back to the apartment. I still keep that *daruma*."

After wandering around the Sanno for about a half hour, we left and went back to Akasaka Mitsuke station.

"Where are we headed now?" I asked.

"Shibuya station. There's something there I want you to see."

Sam was right about trains being the best way to get around Tokyo. While we were at ground level, I had noticed that the bumper-to-bumper traffic had looked like a parking lot. But the trains had no gridlock. They were fast, efficient, and on time.

When we arrived at Shibuya, there was a small crowd of people standing quietly near the entrance of Shibuya station. They were all standing, respectfully, with their hands folded in front of them, in front of a statue of a dog.

"That's Hachiko," Sam explained. "We can actually see the statue better from that coffee shop," she said, pointing to a second-floor coffee shop across the street.

We went to the coffee shop and sat at a small table right up against the front window. From that vantage point, I could see over the crowd that had encircled the statue, and I could clearly see a bronze statue of a dog in the "sit" position.

"Hachiko was an Akita, a dog native to Japan. The Akita is known for its fierce loyalty. There have actually been cases where Akita have protected their owners from bear attacks in the northern island of Hokkaido."

"Hachiko belonged to a university professor. She accompanied him to the train station every day when he went to work, and was always waiting for him when he arrived back at the station at the end of the day. One day, the professor had a heart attack and died while he was at work."

"Hachiko went to the station that day, but he wasn't on the usual train. Hachiko went back to that station every day, waiting all day for her master. She never missed a day. After a few years, she died, always waiting at the station for her master."

"The reason there's a statue for Hachiko is because she represents the virtue that is most important to the Japanese, and to me – loyalty."

I was really moved by the story. As I looked back toward the statue, I could see some of the people wiping their eyes. Obviously, Hachiko represented something very important to them.

"I had a boyfriend, named Dan, in college, after I missed my chance to meet you," Sam said, with a smile.

Then she looked more serious. "He went to Harvard Law also, and we lived together the first year of law school. But there was something about him that really troubled me. For a long time I couldn't put my finger on it, until I thought about Hachiko."

"Ham, Dan didn't have loyalty. His draft number came up, his country needed him, and he didn't answer the call. He ended up running away to Canada. They don't draft women, so I can't really know what goes on inside a guy's head when he gets drafted, but I think I know what I would have done if I did get drafted."

"The United States has given us such an incredible gift as citizens. I think a lot of people don't give it much thought. But I think about it every day. In law school I studied the Constitution, and I studied a lot of history. It was Thomas Jefferson who said 'The tree of liberty must be watered from time to time with the blood of patriots and tyrants.' When Dan was talking about dodging the draft, I lost all respect for him."

"People like you, the people who didn't run away, show the greatest degree of loyalty to our country that's possible. Every GI signs a blank check, payable to the United States, drawn in an amount up to and including his life. I respect that immensely."

"And, more than that," she continued, "I want to be part of it. Don't tell Daddy, but I signed up to join the Air Force."

I didn't know what to say. I'd been listening in rapt attention, and now I was speechless.

"I'm scheduled to start Officer Training School in early October, and by Christmas I'll be an Air Force officer," she continued. "I already have my follow-on assignment to the Judge Advocate General Office at Fifth Air Force Headquarters, at Yokota Air Base. And, because I'll be a JAG, I'll be starting out as a Captain."

"You're going to outrank me," I quipped. "Stand up and let me salute you."

She stood up, and I walked around the table to be face-to-face with her. But I didn't salute her. I gave her a deep hug, and I didn't want to let go.

42

July 28, 1969

The five days of R&R had gone by way too fast, and I didn't want it to end. Sam had shown me around more of Tokyo than I could have imagined, and Tom and Miyako had treated me like family. I found it hard to believe how close I felt to Sam after such a short time. And I felt close enough to discuss my feelings with her.

“Let's not rush things, Ham. We've both made some mistakes in the past. I want to do it right this time.”

She was right, of course. I'd heard the term “rebound”, and it was possible, though not likely, that's all it was. But I didn't think so.

Sam had my address, and I had her phone number. We would just have to wait and see where our relationship went. And I was really anxious to see if it would be possible to place a MARS call from DaNang to Tokyo.

It was time, too soon, to return to Vietnam. These last five days had been exactly what I needed to get my head on straight.

Tom, Miyako and Sam drove me to Yokota Air Base for my return flight. The limo had three rows of seats. The driver was up front, and Tom and Miyako were in the second bench seat. Sam and I sat alone in the back seat, holding hands. She was leaning her head on my shoulder.

When we arrived at the main gate I got out of the limo and went up to the guard. Even though I was in uniform, I still had to show my military identification, and I got a visitor pass that allowed our vehicle to enter the base. I was really grateful Miyako had sent my uniform off to be cleaned and pressed, because I really wanted to look sharp as I escorted Tom, Miyako and Sam around the base. We took a circuitous route to the Passenger Terminal.

Tom looked around, sizing up the real estate.

“I think you're going to like it here, Sam,” he remarked.

Sam sat bolt upright, pulled her hand away from mine, and shot me a look that could kill.

I mouthed the words, “I didn't tell him!”.

“Ease off on him, Sam,” Tom remarked, glancing back over his shoulder. “I figured it out myself. And I'm really proud of you.”

Sam reached over and gave my hand a squeeze.

When we arrived at the terminal, we all went in together. My "new family" was going to wait with me until my flight boarded.

We went into the snack bar, got some sandwiches and coffee, and sat at a table, saying very little. The time passed too quickly.

And then it was time to go.

This was a tough goodbye. I hadn't cried when I left for Vietnam the first time. This was different.

Miyako gave me a big hug, and then reached into her purse and produced a small box, beautifully wrapped.

"This is *omiyage*, from our family to you. Prease think of us when you look at it."

I hadn't been aware of her accent until now. Tom had previously mentioned that she only had a noticeable accent when she was emotional.

I gave Tom and Miyako a big hug, then I gave Sam a long, passionate kiss.

And then I was gone.

43

July 29, 1969

I was pensive the entire flight back to DaNang. I couldn't stop thinking about my time in Japan, and about Sam.

Shortly after takeoff, once the seatbelt sign had been turned off, I got up and retrieved my carry-on bag from the overhead compartment. I removed the small box Miyako had given me from my bag, and carefully unwrapped it, not wanting to damage the delicate paper. I opened the box and looked inside.

It was a small *daruma*, about three inches high. There were no eyes painted on it.

Yet.

44

August 1. 1969

I checked in for the 2100 departure a little early. I wanted to get a thorough Intel briefing before going out on my first flight since returning from R&R.

And I wanted to take care of some personal business. I wrote a short note to Don Springer:

"Don – Sorry I missed you when you came through DaNang. I just returned from R&R, and hope to meet up with you next time you're here, or when I get to NKP. Stay safe.

Ham"

I put the note in an envelope, addressed it, and handed it to our Admin clerk. "Sarge, could you get this into the mailbag going to NKP? Thanks."

Pops Carter was my FAN. When we reviewed the reports from TFA, we could see that there was heavy traffic headed south toward the intersection at Delta 17, and none headed south afterwards. Clearly, there was going to be a large truck park somewhere in the vicinity of Delta 17.

Moonbeam had been advised to have air assets for us on short notice if we needed them, which was likely.

It was just starting to turn dark as I approached the airplane. I always considered the 2100 departure the best night flying period. There was still enough light to perform a really thorough preflight inspection, and by the time we would take off the sun would already be behind the mountains, so we wouldn't be staring into it the whole time we headed west.

And it was a perfect opportunity to let our eyes slowly adapt to night. Not like when we got the midnight launch, and had to instantly go from the brightly-lit Ops building to the pitch-black ramp. Yeah, I liked this a lot.

Right after we departed, I got a call from Covey Ops on fox mike.

“Covey 218, Ops.”

“Go ahead Ops, Covey 218.”

"Roger Covey 218. Right after you took off, we received a call on the land line from Japan. There was a Samantha Marcos calling for you. I'll be damned if I can figure out how she got our number. Anyway, I told her to call back in about five hours.”

“Thanks, Ops. Covey 218 out.” I hadn't given Sam our squadron phone number, since it was classified. That Sam was one resourceful gal. All of a sudden, I was anxious to get this mission over with.

As we headed toward the AO, Pops fine-tuned the starlight scope's focus by homing in on some ground flares we could see off in the distance to the north. He was a real professional, and this was going to be a good mission.

When we entered the AO I selected AUX fuel tanks and started a VR pattern, putting the trail off to our right, so Pops could get a good line of sight with the starlight scope.

Just as we approached Delta 17, Pops shouted, “I've got movers!”

I could see Pops plotting the target as I called Moonbeam on VHF to request air. “Moonbeam, this is Covey 218, request immediate air assets at Delta 17. Prefer Mark 82 and CBU if available.”

“Roger, Covey 218, we have Gunfighter 33 headed your way, ETA 7 minutes. Strike frequency Bravo.”

Damn, those Moonbeam guys were on the ball. I checked my frequency card and tuned the strike frequency on UHF.

Less than a minute later, I heard the Gunfighters check in.

“Gunfighter 33 check.”

“Gunfighter 34.”

“Hello Covey, Gunfighter 33 flight of two fox fours, Mark 82s and CBU 24s. ETA 5 minutes, 10 minutes playtime. Currently at angels 21.”

This guy really had his shit together.

I held my Cadnica flashlight up to my KAK wheel to get an authentication code.

“Roger, Gunfighter, authenticate Alpha Whiskey.”

He came back immediately, “Charlie.”

Okay, we got that out of the way. I knew he was one of the good guys.

I looked over at my FAN. “Pops, do you have a good plot?”

In the dark I could see him nod.

“What's the elevation?”

He was well ahead of me. “5280 feet. Hell, we might be bombing Denver!”

I had Pops guide my eyes to the target, and set up to drop two log markers. I made a long run from west to east, passed over the target and pickled off two ground marking logs five seconds apart. Then I made a wide, sweeping turn to the right.

“Okay, Pops, how'd I do?”

Pops looked through his starlight scope and carefully studied the target. “Hamfist, you have the target bracketed. The target is between the logs, one third of the way from the west mark to the east mark.”

“Got it.” I went back to strike frequency. “Gunfighter, what's your status?”

“We're approaching the target now. We have two lights on the ground. What's your angels, Covey?”

"I'm at angels niner. Target elevation is 5300 feet. I have two marks three hundred meters apart, oriented west to east. The target is one hundred meters east of the western mark. I want you to make your run from north to south with a west break. Mark 82s first, and then we'll save the CBUs for any reaction we get. I'll be holding east of the target."

I turned to Pops. "Pops, are you okay with going christmas tree for a few seconds?"

"Sure, Hamfist. Who do you think I am? Tightass?"

I guess word had gotten around about my last flight.

"Gunfighter, I'm going to go christmas tree for a few seconds so you can get a visual on me."

I flipped on my strobe light and nav lights for about one second, then turned them off and made a hard turn to the north to keep the target and fighter's line of attack in sight.

"Okay, Covey, I have a visual on you...Covey, break, break, break, strela, strela, strela!"

I put my head on a swivel and looked left rear, left front, right front. Nothing. Then the hair on the back of my neck stood up, and I felt like I was moving my head through molasses as I turned to look at my five o'clock right rear.

There was a corkscrewing bright white light approaching me faster than anything I had ever seen.

Then there was a brilliant flash of light, a spine-crushing jolt and a deafening explosion.

And everything went black.

45

August 1, 1969

I think I came to fairly quickly. I had a splitting headache, my ears were ringing, and I had blurry, double vision. I felt dizzy, and I wasn't sure if it was from the explosion or from the violent rocking movement of the airplane.

I was being pressed against the left sidewall of the cockpit in a pulsating manner, with very strong g-forces alternating with almost complete weightlessness. The electrical system of the aircraft was totally gone, and I couldn't see any of the instruments, not that it would have done any good.

I squinted and looked over to where Pops had been sitting and saw a huge, gaping hole. The right aircraft door was gone, and Pops's seat was missing, along with the entire floor area where the seat had been. As I looked through the hole in the floor, I saw, alternatively, the black void beneath the aircraft, then the spinning sky. I was in an undulating, violent spin, and it was becoming ever more violent, with g-forces pushing me ever harder against the left sidewall.

The only illumination in the cockpit was coming from the flames on the right side of the fuselage. The entire right wing was missing, and there was a sheet of flame blowing forward from the right wing root, moving from aft to forward along the right side of the fuselage. The flames were pulsing with the movement of the airplane, at times totally disappearing and then suddenly obscuring the entire area of the right doorway.

I had no idea how high I was, but I knew my chances of getting out were dwindling with every cycle of the tumbling spin. I released my seatbelt and shoulder harness and grabbed the right side of my seat, twisting my body so that my feet were firmly planted against the left sidewall. The right side of my seat was wet and sticky, and I could tell it was blood. I didn't know if it was Pops's or mine. At this point, it didn't matter.

As the G-forces temporarily lessened, I pushed my legs against the left sidewall with all my might and dove down through the hole in the floor.

And tumbled out into the black night.

The adventure continues . .

Follow the adventures of Hamfist Hancock here at:

http://www.hamfistadventures.com/.

Stay in touch with the author via:

Twitter: http://twitter.com/#!/gnolly

Web: http://www.genolly.com

If you liked *Hamfist Over the Trail*, please post a review at Amazon, and let your friends know about the Hamfist Hancock series. Hamfist's adventures continue in *Hamfist Down!*

And stand by for *Hamfist Over Hanoi*, coming soon.

Other books by G. E. Nolly:

Hamfist Down!

This Is Your Captain Speaking: Insider Air Travel Secrets

This Is Your Captain Speaking: Layover Security For Road Warriors

ABOUT THE AUTHOR

George Nolly served as a pilot in the United States Air Force, flying 315 combat missions on two successive tours of duty in Vietnam, flying O-2A and F-4 aircraft. In 1983, George received Tactical Air Command Instructor of the Year Award for his service as an instructor in the Air Force Forward Air Controller course.

Following his Air Force duty, he hired on with United Airlines and rose to the position of B-777 Check Captain. He also served as a Federal Flight Deck Officer. Following his retirement from United, George accepted a position as a B-777 Captain with Jet airways, operating throughout Europe, Asia and the Middle East.

In 2000, George was selected as a Champion in the Body-for-LIFE Transformation Challenge, and is a Certified Fitness Trainer and self-defense expert with more than 30 years' experience in combative arts.

George received a Bachelor of Science Degree from the United States Air Force Academy and received a Master of Science Degree, in Systems Management, from the University of Southern California. He completed all of the required studies for a second Master of Science Degree, in Education, at the University of Southern California, and received his Doctor of Business Administration Degree, specializing in Homeland Security, from Northcentral University. He now flight instructs in the B777 and B787.